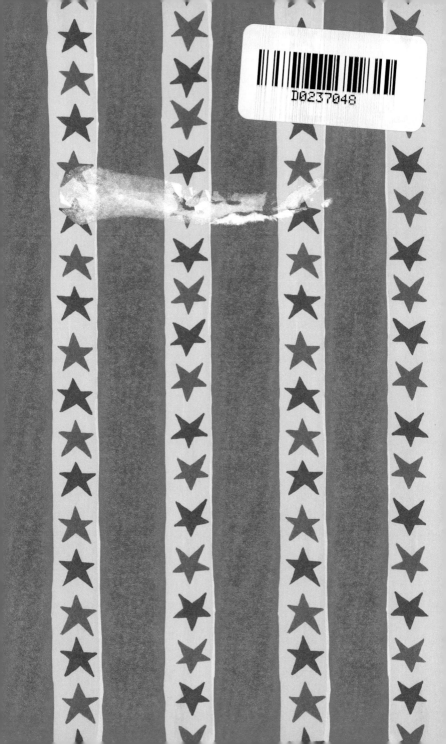

A LAURA MARLIN MYSTERY

KENTUCKY THRILLER

Also by Lauren St John

Laura Marlin Mysteries

Dead Man's Cove
Kidnap in the Caribbean

The White Giraffe Quartet

The White Giraffe
Dolphin Song
The Last Leopard
The Elephant's Tale

The One Dollar Horse Trilogy

The One Dollar Horse

A LAURA MARLIN MYSTERY

KENTUCKY THRILLER

Lauren St John

Illustrated by David Dean

Orion
Children's Books

First published in Great Britain in 2012
by Orion Children's Books
a division of the Orion Publishing Group Ltd
Orion House
5 Upper St Martin's Lane
London WC2H 9EA
An Hachette UK Company

1 3 5 7 9 10 8 6 4 2

A catalogue record for this book is available
from the British Library

ISBN 978 1 4440 0022 1

Printed in Great Britain by Clays Ltd, St Ives plc

www.laurenstjohn.com

www.orionbooks.co.uk

*For Thomas Beattie, whose beautiful thoroughbreds
(Troubleshooter especially) so inspired me as a child*

THE HORSEBOX WAS lying on its side when they came over the rise. Afterwards, it occurred to Laura Marlin that if they'd done one thing differently that morning their story would have been someone else's story, only it would have had another ending entirely, and who's to say whether that ending would have been good or bad.

Laura had a theory that life was like a passage and how things turned out depended on which doors you opened or which ones opened for you. For instance, fate could have decreed that she remain forever at Sylvan Meadows Children's Home, where she'd lived since her mum had died giving birth to her. Even now she could have been in her old room overlooking the car park, longing for a life of excitement and adventure like the characters in her books while in reality having nothing to look forward to but another meal of glutinous porridge or bleached vegetables.

Instead, a door in the corridor of Laura's desperately dull existence had blown wide open and who should be waiting on the other side but Calvin Redfern, her mother's brother. He was a fisheries inspector with the handsome but slightly careworn looks of the hero of an old black and white movie. When he'd learned of her existence five months earlier, he'd immediately come forward to claim her. Before Laura knew it, she was living at number 28 Ocean View Terrace in the beautiful seaside town of St Ives, Cornwall, had adopted a three-legged husky named Skye, and was up to her ears in all the adventures she could handle.

That was how she'd met Tariq, a Bengali boy from Bangladesh in South Asia, who'd become her best friend. They were the same age, but where Laura had a cap of pale blonde hair and peaches and cream skin, Tariq was the colour of burnt honey, with glossy black hair shaved short at the back. His brutal childhood as a slave, first in a quarry in his home country and later in St Ives until he was rescued by Laura, had left him thin but very strong, and was responsible for the shadows that sometimes showed in his tiger's eyes before his easy laugh chased them away again.

Tariq and Laura did everything together and for that reason he was the first person she called when her uncle woke up on that sparkling Saturday in April and spontaneously decided they should go to Sennen Cove for a picnic. That should have set the scene for a perfect day, but almost immediately a series of things conspired to delay them.

First, Tariq was twenty minutes late. As he was leaving his foster parents' home near Carbis Bay, a car screeched up and he had to help his foster father, Rob Ashworth, a vet, with a cat emergency.

Next, Skye slipped his lead as Laura was coaxing him into the car. He went racing down the road after a seagull while their eccentric neighbour, Mrs Crabtree, yelled approval. That had held them up for a further eight minutes, and they lost more time still when they drove away without the picnic basket and had to return for it.

All of which meant that they were approximately thirty-six minutes later than they'd intended to be as they twisted through the sunny lanes past fields dotted with sheep. That didn't matter since they weren't on a schedule, but it was the reason Laura's uncle decided to take a shortcut. 'It's such a beautiful day that it seems a shame to waste a second of it,' he'd said. Shortly afterwards, they flew over a blind hill into a shadowed copse and almost crashed into the horsebox.

If it wasn't for the fact that former Chief Inspector Redfern had taken part in numerous high-speed pursuits in years gone by when he was Scotland's most famous detective and thus had lightning reactions, they'd have had a head-on collision. As it was the children were slammed hard against their seatbelts as he braked, swerved and brought the car to a skidding halt beneath a canopy of dark

3

trees. An overnight shower had made the road slicker than an oil spill.

When Laura opened her eyes, he was staring down at her anxiously.

'Laura, are you all right? You've had quite a scare. Thank goodness you and Tariq were strapped in. If something had happened to you both, I'd never have forgiven myself. Skye, are you okay? If you're still capable of washing my face, I guess you are. Well done, Laura, for hanging on to him.'

Laura clambered from the car, bruised, cold and shaky. She leaned on Skye and he whined and licked her hand. Tariq was pale beneath his dark skin. For a good two minutes nobody spoke. Calvin Redfern dug the flask out of the picnic basket and poured them each a cup of hot, sweet coffee 'for the shock'. He gave Skye a couple of dog biscuits. Then the trio stood in the green gloom, regarding the horsebox that could have killed them as if it were a hostile spacecraft that had landed in their path with the sole intention of harming them.

'You can tell from the skid marks what's happened,' Calvin Redfern explained, breaking the silence. 'The driver swerved to avoid something – a rabbit or a deer – and the trailer hitch snapped off, causing the horsebox to overturn. It's an ancient thing, barely roadworthy. I dread to think what sort of injuries the pony or donkey or whatever was in there sustained. Presumably the owner was unhurt because he or she managed to drive away, as you can tell from the muddy tracks.

'I'm surprised your foster father didn't get a call, Tariq.

4

He's one of the best vets around. Then again, maybe the horsebox was empty. Probably was since I can't see any hoof prints. At any rate, it would have been helpful if the driver had phoned the incident in so that the police could have towed the damaged box out of the road. We need to act fast to prevent a serious accident. Laura, would you mind if I borrowed your red sweatshirt? You can wear my jumper. You're in shock and I don't want you getting a chill.'

As Laura shrugged out of her top, he found a stout stick and stripped it of its leaves. Tying the sweatshirt to one end, he handed it to Tariq. 'Son, I need your help. While I call the police, would you mind standing at the top of the rise and waving this as a red flag warning if any vehicles approach? Make sure you stand safely on the side of the road. There's plenty of visibility coming the other way, so I think the blind hill is our main concern.'

As the boy hurried away, Calvin leaned against his car and took out his mobile phone. 'Laura, would you be good enough to call out the number plate of the horsebox when I get through to the police?'

'No problem.' Yet as Laura walked towards the fallen horsebox with Skye, she felt oddly scared. Overhead, the twisting grey branches of the trees laced together like hands, their dense black foliage muffling the birdsong and shutting out the sunshine. As she circled the horsebox, noting the cracked old tyres, buckled mudguards and caved-in rear, something struck her as strange. There *was* no number plate. In the place where it should have been was an empty slot. Curiously, the area around it was free

5

of dust, almost as if the driver had wiped it clean after the accident. A couple of screws lay on the ground nearby.

'Hold on a minute, Pete,' her uncle was saying into his phone. He put his hand over the mouthpiece. 'What is it, Laura?'

'There is none. No number plate, I mean.'

'What do you mean? Has it fallen off in the crash?' He marched over to her. She saw surprise register on his face. He took in the screws on the ground and the polished bumper. 'Pete, there's something wrong here. The plate's gone and it seems as if someone's gone to a fair amount of effort to erase any fingerprints. I'll take a look and call you back. In the meantime, I'd appreciate it if you could send that tow truck right away.'

The last three words were almost drowned out by a blood-curdling growl from Skye, who was sniffing the horsebox. This was followed almost immediately by a dull thud.

Calvin Redfern went still. 'I don't believe it.'

'I think I saw something move!' cried Laura, crouching down and peering into the darkness of the box. 'Uncle Calvin, there's a pony inside. I think it's still alive.'

Two violent thuds followed, rocking the trailer. 'Alive and kicking by the sound of things.' Calvin Redfern hit the speed dial on his phone. 'I'm calling Rob Ashworth. We need a vet urgently. Laura, take Skye to the car and lock him in. We don't want him frightening the creature any more than it already has been.'

By the time Laura returned, splinters were flying. She bent down and tried talking to the pony in a soothing

6

voice. It worked until two cars drove through the tunnel of trees. Flagged down by Tariq, they drove relatively slowly, but one had music blaring and didn't bother turning it down. The animal started kicking harder than ever.

Calvin Redfern checked his watch. 'It'll be at least ten minutes before Rob gets here. We're going to have to try to help the poor creature before it injures itself any further. Laura, help me try to pull the side back. It's in a wretched state, this horsebox. It wouldn't surprise me if the driver fled the scene because he didn't want to be held responsible. He probably thought the horse was dead.'

'Maybe he was a horse thief,' suggested Laura, pulling with all her strength at the wooden planks that held the box together. She felt one give.

Despite the situation, her uncle laughed as he tackled a screw with his penknife. 'You read too many Matt Walker novels,' he teased, alluding to the fictional detective inspector who was Laura's hero. 'You're always looking for mysteries to solve. It's not that horse thieves don't exist. There are plenty about, make no mistake about that, just not around here. I doubt the Cornish police are overburdened with reports of abandoned stolen ponies on idyllic country lanes.'

'But why else would the driver have gone away and simply left it?' asked Laura, jumping back as a hoof struck the side of the box again, showering her with splinters.

'There could be a million reasons. Maybe he'd been drinking. Perhaps he was uninsured. The pony was silent when we got here, which probably means it was unconscious. The owner might have assumed it was either

7

fatally injured or dead and decided that he or she didn't want to pay the vet bills. There are any number of reasons.'

A pickup truck rattled over the hill, its headlights pushing back the shadows. It squeaked to a halt beside them and a man with the ruddy, weather-beaten face of a fisherman or farmer leaned from the window. 'Need any help, mate?'

Whatever was in the horsebox launched a final assault on the sagging wood. The side exploded, like a boat disintegrating under the onslaught of a hurricane. Tariq came running down the road. 'What's going on? It sounded as if a bomb went off.'

There was a squeal of rage and the creature beneath the wood stirred and gathered itself. Laura caught a glimpse of a chestnut ear and a length of dusty mane before the beast gathered itself and surged to its feet, shaking off debris like a phoenix emerging from the ashes.

She gasped. In the white glow of headlights, the coat of the stallion was all flash and fire, his flaring nostrils scarlet. Every inch of him rippled with muscle. He stood on the wreckage of the horsebox, statuesque in his perfection, gazing at them with a mixture of terror and pride.

Calvin Redfern exhaled. 'I'm not an expert but I will say one thing. That's no pony.'

~2~

UUUUUUUUUUU

'**IF WE CAN'T FIND** his owner, can we keep him?'

Laura hung over the fence and gazed adoringly at the red stallion as he tore around the field behind the Carbis Bay Riding Centre. In the week since they'd rescued him, she and Tariq had been to visit him every day after school and now it was Saturday and she still couldn't get over how magnificent he was, or that he was temporarily theirs. When the sunlight danced across his coat, little jets of flame seemed to shoot from it. Catching sight of his audience, he swerved in their direction and came to a prancing halt. Laura offered him an apple. He took it from her delicately.

A smile tugged at the corner of Calvin Redfern's mouth. 'No. We absolutely can't keep him.'

Laura wiped her hands on her jeans. In her experience, grown-ups mostly said no without thinking. It was their first response and Laura rarely accepted it without question. 'Why not?'

He laughed. 'How many reasons do you want me to give you? For one thing, I can't afford it on a fisheries investigator's salary. We've been taking care of him for a mere seven days and he's already cost a king's ransom in medicine and food and livery charges. If it weren't for Rob's generosity in treating him for free, I'd be bankrupt. But it's not just that. Who would exercise him? You and Tariq? Me? I'd sooner face down a gang of armed robbers.'

Laura knew what he meant. Over the past week she'd spent many happy hours daydreaming about forming a unique bond with the red stallion, one which would result in her being able to gallop him bareback through the surf on Porthmeor Beach in St Ives, the envy of all. She'd imagined sitting in tandem with Tariq on the horse's high red back as he carried them through poppy-scattered meadows or along the cliff path past Dead Man's Cove, Skye loping by his side.

At the same time, she was quite intimidated by the stallion. He towered over her. Jeanette, the stable girl, said that he was close to 17 hands high. Apart from a few minor cuts and bruises and a slightly swollen fetlock, now healed, he'd suffered remarkably few ill effects from the accident. When he tore across the field, his great hooves seemed to eat up the ground at a furious pace. There was something gloriously wild and almost dangerous about him.

'Are you listening to a word I'm saying?' demanded her uncle, his tone exasperated.

'Of course I am,' said Laura, not altogether truthfully. She caught Tariq's eye as he handed the horse a couple of carrots and grinned. She knew that he too had been fantasising about a summer holiday full of adventures with the red stallion and the husky and that if there was anyone who could turn that fantasy into reality it was her best friend. His foster dad was always saying that Tariq had a way with animals. Something about him seemed to make them happy.

Calvin Redfern sighed. 'Laura, do you really believe that a horse that looks like this, a thoroughbred worthy of a king, has no owner?'

'Well, no, but maybe his owner couldn't afford to keep him, or had no insurance and was worried about the vet bill if he was injured.'

Her uncle rubbed the horse behind his ears. The red stallion tilted his head on one side and looked positively soppy. 'Possibly, but what's much more likely is that he's been kidnapped, possibly for a ransom of some kind.'

Laura stared at him. 'I thought you said that the Cornish police weren't exactly overburdened with cases of abandoned stolen ponies.'

He smiled. 'That's true. I did. But that was before the St Ives police rang me with the results of the forensic tests on the horsebox.'

Laura craned forward so eagerly that she nearly fell off the fence. The red stallion rubbed his head against her and she lost her fight with gravity. She landed on her feet, laughing. 'And . . . ?'

'Well, there are none.'

'You mean they didn't find any evidence?' said Tariq. 'No fingerprints or DNA?'

'Not a thing. It had been wiped completely clean. Tellingly, the serial number on the chassis of the horsebox had been removed – a favourite trick of vehicle thieves. And, judging by that little nick on the horse's neck, the microchip that would have identified him has been removed. But here's what's peculiar. My detective friend, Pete Watson, has trawled the stolen horse database, and I've made a couple of discreet enquiries in the horse racing world via a friend of mine who is head of security at one of the biggest racetracks. No horse matching the red stallion's description has been reported missing.'

The subject of their discussion tossed his head, wheeled and burst into a flat out gallop. Round the field he swept, ears pricked, running for the sheer joy of it.

Tariq was awestruck by his tremendous speed. 'Hard to believe no one would notice if a horse like that vanished.'

'If that beast carries on tearing up my good grass like that, I'll be charging you extra,' warned Vicky Pendleton, a hefty woman with a swinging brown bob and cheerful face. 'Trouble is, I don't have any stables free at the moment. I was going to suggest that you move him to Tip Top Riding Centre over near Penzance, but they had a break-in last night, which doesn't exactly inspire confidence.'

Calvin Redfern, leaning against the fence watching the horse, glanced round. 'Tip Top Riding Centre? You mean the most rundown stables in Cornwall. That place is one stiff breeze away from collapsing in a heap. What were the thieves after? Rusty nails? A bridle held together with string?'

'Hard to say. Nothing was taken. Third in a row, though – well, one was a farm but it was the same story.'

'Third what in a row?' prompted Laura.

Vicky pursed her lips. 'Third break-in in three nights at an equestrian centre. Two riding schools and Hidden Bounty farm, which runs pony trekking holidays. In each case nothing was taken and none of the horses were harmed so the only people who called the police were the owners of Tip Top. The constable who visited told them it was probably teenagers out for a laugh or lazy burglars.'

Laura thought: Or the driver of the horsebox in search of his red stallion. There was a glint in her uncle's eyes and she wondered if he was thinking the same thing. 'What do you think these lazy burglars are after?'

Vicky had her hands on her hips. 'Well, if it's money they want they'll be sorely disappointed if they come looking for it here. The way business is going, they'll be lucky if they can find any loose change down the back of the sofa. Still I'm not going to take any chances with my horses. For the next few nights, my twin nephews are going to guard the place.'

She nodded towards the car park, where a multi-coloured VW van was pulling in. Out climbed two young men with salt-crinkled surfer hair. Their biceps and chests bulged as if they'd been blown up with bicycle pumps.

Calvin Redfern did a double take. 'Good grief, Vicky,

ind of trouble are you expecting? An armed gang? en trained Ninjas.'

tter safe than sorry,' Vicky told him as she strode away to greet her nephews, Sam and Scott 'They're both black belts in karate. Bruce Lee himself couldn't get past them.'

Laura was of the opinion that the more burly bodyguards the red stallion had the better. She couldn't bear the idea of the horse being stolen again, particularly by the thieves who'd nearly killed him with their reckless driving. She was about to ask her uncle for his opinion on the riding centre break-ins when Tariq said: 'What's that on your T-shirt, Laura?'

'Where?' Laura examined her front, expecting to see a brown stain. To the despair of Rowenna, their housekeeper, she spilled her morning cup of coffee with monotonous regularity.

'Try the back.'

Her uncle turned her round so he could inspect the damage. 'Laura, what on earth have you been doing? You have chestnut stripes across your shoulders. You look like an escaped tiger. Where . . . ? Ohhh . . .'

His eyes met Tariq's and they both turned to gaze at the red stallion sauntering towards them, dark with sweat after his run.

Laura knew what they were thinking. The horse had rubbed his head against her. If he'd left chestnut marks behind, there could be only one explanation. She reached out a hand and rubbed the horse's forehead. A few bright chestnut hairs came loose. The base of the hair was snow white. 'His face has been dyed to disguise his identity,' she cried excitedly. 'He has a star or something.'

'That confirms he's been stolen,' said Tariq.

Calvin Redfern frowned. 'That would seem to be the case. What we have to discover is why and by whom?'

He stopped abruptly. 'Listen to me. I'm talking as if I'm still a detective when all I do these days is arrest fishermen who catch too many fish. And you two are supposed to be having fun and staying out of trouble for once. It's not long since we returned from the Caribbean where you had enough adventures to last you a lifetime. Let's have some peace for a change.'

He held up his hand. 'Don't fret, Laura, I'm going to make a quick call to Detective Watson to tell him that he needs to search for the owner of a red chestnut stallion with a blaze. But then we're going to forget all about it and go on the picnic we missed out on last week. This is a police matter now.'

'But . . . !' Laura protested. She got no further.

Jeanette, the stable girl, came rushing out of the riding centre office, blonde hair streaming behind her. 'Mr Redfern, you'd better come quickly. I think you'll want to see this.'

~ 3 ~

'OUR RED STALLION!' Laura cried in wonder after she, Tariq and her uncle had watched the horse sweep to an epic victory in the Kentucky Derby on Vicky's old TV at Carbis Bay Riding Centre. Calvin Redfern had explained that in the US the race was known as the 'Durby' and not the 'Darby' as it was pronounced in England.

Laura peeked out of the window to double check that the horse was still in Vicky's field and not a figment of her imagination. He was there. His ears were pricked and he was gazing into the distance as if straining to see the faraway home from which he'd been snatched.

On television, the red stallion looked quite different. His

fiery coat was offset by a big white blaze, and his muscles rippled with effort as he surged past the other horses. His name, it turned out, was Gold Rush. Fans called him Goldie.

'And a gold rush he has proved to be for his owners, Americans Blake and Christine Wainright,' the newsreader enthused on the BBC lunchtime news. 'After breaking several track records as a two-year-old, he went on to win the coveted Triple Crown at three, achieving legendary status. Ten days ago, Goldie, as he is known to his fans, now retired at the grand old age of seven and worth \$75 million . . .'

Tariq gasped.

Laura's mouth dropped open. *'Seventy-five million!* For a *horse . . .'*

'Shhh,' scolded Vicky. 'We're trying to listen.'

'. . . was stolen when the lorry in which he was travelling to his Kentucky home in the US was ambushed by masked raiders. Two stable employees were seriously injured trying to stop them. The theft was kept a secret from the media and public while the Wainwrights attempted to negotiate with the kidnappers. On the advice of detectives, the family refused to pay a ransom demand. A week ago, the kidnappers disappeared into thin air. Now Kentucky police are appealing . . .'

A breaking news headline scrolled along the bottom of the screen: REWARD OFFERED FOR SAFE RETURN OF \$75 MILLION KENTUCKY DERBY STAR.

The newsreader turned her attention to a factory fire drama in Scotland and Vicky switched off the TV. Everyone

17

in the office rushed outside to see the red stallion, including the beefy nephews, Sam and Scott.

'Doesn't seem such a silly idea now, getting in reinforcements,' Vicky remarked to Calvin Redfern.

'No,' he agreed. 'It doesn't. And we might need even more. I'll speak to the police about it. We have to try to keep this quiet until Detective Watson can get in touch with Goldie's owners, the Wainwrights, but I doubt we'll be successful. Before you know it, you'll be swamped with reporters. Dozens of cranks will be claiming they own the horse, or trying to collect the reward. But that's not what's worrying me. My concern is that any gang professional enough, and determined enough, to snatch a multi-million dollar racehorse and whisk it across the Atlantic, is likely to try again.'

A chill went through Laura as it occurred to her that the infamous Straight A's were just such a gang. They were professional enough and determined enough to kidnap a famous horse and spirit it across the sea. But she put the thought firmly from her head. The Straight A gang were criminal masterminds. Their cunning schemes usually involved millions or billions of pounds. Twice she and Tariq had got in the way of the Straight A's' wicked plans and twice they'd almost paid with their lives. But it was hard to imagine the gang going to the effort and expense of stealing a horse from America, only to abandon it by the roadside in some battered horsebox.

'Should we hide Goldie in a stable to keep him safe?' Vicky asked.

Laura looked round. 'Wouldn't that make it too easy for

the gang to get him into a corner and catch him if they do slip past your nephews?'

'Plus he might injure himself if he panicked in a confined space,' Tariq put in.

'Mmm, I think Tariq and Laura have a point,' Calvin Redfern told Vicky. 'The field might be the safest place for him, especially if you put a few others horses in with him. He'll have the space to run away if the worst comes to the worst. They'll have a heck of a job to catch him. But hopefully it won't come to that.'

'Would you like me to leave Skye here for added security?' Laura offered, but Vicky drew the line at that. Her aged fox terrier was, she claimed, the best burglar alarm in Cornwall and she refused to have his nose put out of joint by a husky, even if it was one with three legs and a history of spotting villains.

It was a decision she'd soon regret.

The phone call that changed everything had come later that day as they'd walked through the door of number 28 Ocean View Terrace. The picnic had been postponed yet again after they'd discovered the red stallion's true identity, because Calvin Redfern needed to speak to the police and there was Goldie's security to organise. By the time they'd driven back to St Ives, a late afternoon breeze was crinkling the sea around Porthminster Beach. The slowly sinking sun illuminated the shallows and turned them a Greek Island turquoise.

Skye bounded noisily up the steps to greet Rowenna, their housekeeper. He was making such a racket that Laura almost didn't hear the phone ring, but at the last second she managed to grab the receiver.

'Quiet, Skye. Shhh! I'm sorry. Hello?'

'Evenin', ma'am,' drawled a rich, mellow voice. 'My apologies for disturbin' you. It sure sounds as if you have your hands full.'

'Oh, that's just Skye, my husky. He loves life.'

A laugh boomed from the receiver. 'A philosophy of which I heartily approve. Now young lady, I believe you have something that belongs to me. Something very precious. Thanks to your kindness in rescuing him, I'm told you are in possession of my horse, Gold Rush. We call him Goldie. We think of him as family, the same way you probably do about your husky.'

Laura had warmed to Blake Wainright on the phone and she'd done so again when he walked through the door twenty-four hours later, and not just because he made a big fuss of Skye. He was a tall, sinewy man dressed in the type of black suit and flowing white shirt a country singer might wear. As she showed him into the living room, she'd noticed that he had a long, range-walking stride, and that his eyes were the colour of faded jeans with deep smile lines around the corners. He had silver-white hair rippling over his collar, and a perfectly curled moustache. At the end of his long legs, now stretched out in front of him, was a pair of steel-tipped black cowboy boots with red stitching.

'You've heard of Shergar, I presume?'

Laura cupped her chin with her palm and leant forward so she wouldn't miss a single word of Blake's slow, musical drawl. It was an accent that conjured up images from a film she'd seen about America's Deep South. Of treacle-dark bayous overhung with oaks draped in Spanish moss, of alligators blinking in their depths, of white-whiskered black men playing the blues, of plates piled high with pink crawfish, of horse-drawn carts festooned in roses and steamboats on the Mississippi.

But Blake Wainright was not from New Orleans, the subject of the movie. He was from Lexington, Kentucky, a very different corner of the South if the photos on his mobile were anything to go by. They showed fields of lush green grass lined with white fences, behind which dozens of shining thoroughbreds grazed. Lexington was, he'd told them, the heart of the racing industry in the US; birthplace of some of the fastest horses ever to scorch the track.

Among the greatest of these was the red stallion.

'You've heard of Shergar, I presume?' Blake Wainright asked again. Calvin Redfern had gone into his study to call Vicky at the stables, so Laura and Tariq were drinking coffee with the visitor.

Tariq said shyly: 'My foster dad, Rob Ashworth – he's the vet who treated Goldie after the accident – mentioned him last night. When I told him that Gold Rush had been stolen by a gang demanding a ransom, he said: "Shades of Shergar".'

Blake Wainright's moustache twitched. 'Shades of

Shergar indeed. Did he explain further?'

'He said that Shergar was one of the greatest horses in the history of Irish racing – a horse to make your heart sing. He described him as a big bay with four white socks and a blaze and a loving, bombproof personality, and said that some of his wins were so effortless he barely seemed to break out of a canter. He said that to the people of Ireland, Shergar was a national hero.'

'I couldn't have put it better myself.' Blake Wainright's voice was so gravelly that it resonated in Laura's chest. 'Unfortunately for that wonderful horse, fate took a cruel twist. On a foggy winter's night in 1983, masked men in balaclavas drove into Ballymany Stud in County Kildare with a trailer. They tied up the family of his groom, James Fitzgerald, and forced James at gunpoint to load Shergar. The horse was driven away and that was the last anyone ever saw of him.'

Laura was on the edge of her seat. 'He vanished without trace?'

'Without trace. To this day, no one knows what became of him, although there are many theories and some of those involved have confessed anonymously.'

'My uncle would have found Shergar if they'd thought of calling him,' Laura told him loyally. 'He's a fisheries inspector now, but he used to be one of the best detectives in the country – as good as Matt Walker. Matt's a fictional detective but he's a genius.'

Blake Wainright raised an amused eyebrow. 'Is that right? Sounds as if both of them should have been on the case. There was a lot of police bungling – not helped by the fact that eight long hours elapsed before the cops were told that the horse was missing, so vital time and evidence was lost. The gang issued a series of ransom demands, but it soon became clear they'd made a critical error. They believed that the horse was owned by the Aga Khan, one of the richest men in the world. In fact, he was owned by thirty-five shareholders – what's known as a syndicate. Quite correctly, the shareholders refused to pay the ransom and the horse was never seen alive again. To this day, nobody involved in the crime has ever been caught or brought to justice.'

'That's one of the saddest stories I've ever heard,' said Laura. 'Poor Shergar. Can you imagine how terrified and alone he must have felt. When Goldie was stolen, weren't you afraid that the same thing would happen to him?'

Blake Wainright stared hard into his coffee cup. He cleared his throat, his faded blue eyes suddenly moist. 'Like I said, Goldie is family to us. People keep going on about the money, but that's the last thing on my mind. I've hardly slept since the horse was taken. When the police called to say that he'd been found, it was like being handed fifty Christmas presents all at once. I jumped on the first plane from Kentucky to Newquay via London, and caught a taxi to St Ives. So here I am, a bit jet-lagged, but over the moon that my beloved Goldie is safe and well.'

He smiled. 'Speaking of which, as nice as it is to chat to you both, I can't wait to see my horse. When your uncle returns, I'd be very grateful to be taken to him.'

Calvin Redfern strode into the room. Always an imposing figure, his handsome face now looked like the sky over Porthmeor Beach when a sea storm was sweeping in.

'I'm afraid that won't be possible.'

The American leapt to his feet. 'But why not?'

'Because,' Calvin Redfern said, 'the horse is gone.'

~ 4 ~

'*GONE?*'

Blake Wainright's face was as white as his hair. He said faintly: 'How could he possibly be gone? You told me that two cops, a couple of musclemen and the fox terrier reputed to be the best burglar alarm in Cornwall were guarding him. Are you telling me that the kidnappers slipped past them?'

Calvin Redfern looked grim. 'It would appear so. When Vicky arrived at the stables this morning she found her nephews, the two police constables and the dog, sound asleep. It was some time before she could rouse anyone and now she says they're all stumbling around, groggy

25

and with splitting headaches. That would suggest they'd been drugged, although how it was managed no one can think.'

'What happened to the third constable?' asked Laura.

Her uncle stared at her. 'There were only two men on duty last night. I know that because I was with Detective Watson when he assigned them.'

'Laura's right,' confirmed Tariq. 'A third one came later. He held the paddock gate open for us when we went to say a final goodbye to Goldie before leaving yesterday. He had a stone in his shoe so he was bending down and we didn't really see his face, but I noticed that he was youngish – in his early twenties or so. He had blue-black stubble and black hair cut quite short at the back.'

'An inside job?' demanded Blake Wainright. 'Is that what you're telling me? One of the policemen supposedly protecting Goldie has stolen him?'

'Not a real policeman,' Laura said, trying to sound soothing. 'A fake one. He probably volunteered to make coffee or a meal for everyone and slipped sleeping powder into it.'

Calvin Redfern raked his fingers through his greying dark hair. 'I can't tell you how sorry I am, Blake. This is immensely embarrassing for the police. I've left a message for Detective Watson.'

The American had the look of someone who wanted to bang his head against the wall in despair, but he said with spirit, 'No cops! I mean no disrespect, sir, but those morons were no use at all when it came to finding Shergar and now the Cornish police have blown it with Gold Rush.

What I would appreciate, Mr Redfern, is if you could drive me to the stables yourself. I understand that you were once the best detective around. If there's a clue to be found, I'd like you to locate it.'

Calvin Redfern gave Laura and Tariq a hard look. His detective past was something he didn't usually advertise. He opened his mouth as if to refuse, but was conscious that someone had to try to make amends for the policing disaster. 'We'll do our best,' he promised at last.

The field was empty apart from a couple of Shetland ponies. They alone seemed cheerful. Everybody else at the riding school was in a fog of gloom, no one more so than Vicky and her twin nephews, who were nursing sore heads and feeling sorry for themselves. Their bulging muscles and martial arts skills had been no use at all.

'It's as if someone's put my brain through a tumble dryer,' grumbled Sam. 'Last thing I remember is sitting down to eat the pizza that nice constable ordered. After that, I have total amnesia.'

'They'd never have got away with it if I'd been awake,' Scott moaned in frustration. 'A couple of roundhouse kicks and they'd have been begging for mercy.'

'Yes, but you weren't awake, were you,' retorted his brother. 'You were snoring like a dragon with sinusitis. They might have begged you to shut up, but that's about it.'

Scott was indignant. 'Ever heard *yourself*? You sound

like a hippo with flu. Your whole bed shakes. They could measure the vibrations on the Richter scale . . .'

Laura and Tariq left them squabbling and took the husky down to the field. In spite of his objections, Calvin Redfern had persuaded Blake Wainright to speak to Detective Watson, who'd screeched into the riding centre a short time ago, full of apologies.

Laura was determined to find the clue the American so desperately wanted before the police did. She could relate to the anguish he'd clearly felt when her uncle told him that Goldie had gone missing again. If someone stole Skye, she'd be devastated. And yet so far the only clue was a few tyre tracks, which, Calvin Redfern said, had been made by the most commonly used tyres in the United Kingdom, so were not much use as a clue at all.

She stood by the gate and did her best to think like her hero, Detective Inspector Matt Walker. Laura's dream was to be a great detective when she was older and when she wasn't pestering her uncle about the methods he'd used to solve cases, she spent hours combing the pages of her Matt Walker novels for tips.

In *The Case of the Missing Heiress*, Matt had observed that quite often in kidnappings the solution was in front of investigators' eyes, but they spent so much time working on complicated theories that they missed the blindingly obvious. Laura unclipped Skye's leash. He was straining to explore the field. She tried to decide where to start searching for clues. Matt believed that every crime scene told a story. It was simply a matter of knowing how to read it.

While Tariq searched the field with Skye, Laura studied

the tyre tracks. They led to the five-barred gate, where the thieves appeared to have parked to make the loading of the horse as easy as possible. There were distinct tracks on the approach to the field and a flurry of hoofprints and boot marks just inside it.

'Wellingtons,' Calvin Redfern had said ruefully of the bootprints, prodding one with a stick. 'Only about ten million sold every year.'

If the footprints and tyre treads told no story, maybe the pattern of them – what Matt Walker called 'tracking psychology' – would. The vehicle had driven directly to the gate, but departed erratically, turning in a wide loop and zooming away in a zigzag. Even if they were in a hurry, it didn't make sense that the thieves would transport a multi-million dollar horse in such a dangerous manner.

Unless . . .

Laura stared at the chaos of prints and churned up earth. Unless the horse wasn't on board when they sped away.

She considered the circumstances. Rob Ashworth had once commented that horses lived by their memories. A stallion with the strength and speed of Gold Rush, a highly strung horse who found himself approached or seized in the dead of night by men he associated with a series of negative or painful events, would not willingly allow himself to be led into another horsebox, particularly when his experience in the last one had been so traumatic.

Across the field, Tariq was with Skye. The husky was sniffing at a fence post.

'Tariq,' called Laura, breaking into a run. 'Check for hoofprints, deep ones, on the other side of the fence.'

Even before she reached him, he was giving her the thumbs up. Goldie might have vanished again, but this time at least he was free.

~ 5 ~

'I **DON'T WANT** to rain on your parade, but I'm telling you now, there's more to this kidnapped stallion business than meets the eye,' Mrs Crabtree told Laura. 'Always is in the racing game. It's a magnet for chancers, gamblers, criminals and dreamers. The pretty horses, the rainbow jockey silks, the fancy hats of the ladies who go to watch, they're just the window dressing. Behind the scenes, there are tricks going on that would be the envy of any conjurer. Big money involved, you see. Wherever there are millions at stake, there'll be men trying to make even more and they'll do whatever it takes. Sleight of hand, smoke and mirrors, rabbits out of hats, you name it, they'll have it up their sleeves.'

Laura sat on her neighbour's stone wall trying to keep a big grin off her face and only half-listening. She was watching Skye who in turn was watching the surfers bob like seals on the heaving blue-grey surf a few hundred metres below. The horizon was peach-pink with the setting sun. Usually by this time she'd be ravenous and in the kitchen pestering their housekeeper, Rowenna, to hurry up with dinner, but tonight she wanted to linger in the sea air and savour the excitement of the day.

It had been harder than expected to convince Detective Watson and the other grown-ups that the red stallion had escaped from the Carbis Bay riding centre rather than been stolen.

'Nonsense,' barked Vicky, unwilling to admit that a $75 million horse might have got out of her field. 'That fence is a metre and a half high. He would have to have the leaping power of a champion show jumper to get over it.'

'Or be very afraid,' Tariq pointed out.

Vicky ignored him. 'Besides, any thief cunning enough to trick four men and a dog into eating a pizza loaded with sleeping powder would have thought to bring tranquilisers to sedate the horse if he was giving trouble.'

Laura shrugged. 'Maybe the gang never managed to get close enough to inject him or knock him out with chloroform or whatever else they were planning. Goldie probably took one look at them, remembered what happened the last time they grabbed him, and bolted for his life.'

And so it had proved. Thanks to Skye, the search party

had been out on the moors for barely twenty minutes when they found the red stallion grazing happily on a hillock. Blake Wainright was beside himself with joy. Only problem was, no one could get close to the horse. Every time they drew near enough to see the whites of his eyes, he raced away, tail held high – though whether through fright or because he was revelling in his newfound freedom, it was hard to tell. Laura suspected the latter.

'He always did have a mind of his own,' admitted the American, his elation at finding Goldie subsiding as the day wore on and the search party pursued the stallion up and down gullies, across a stream and through a thicket of gorse. They'd attempted to send two riders after him, but the barrel-bellied trekking cobs had no hope of matching his effortless blasts of speed.

'It's a game to him,' panted Vicky, crossly plucking thorns out of her jodhpurs. It had started to drizzle and everyone in the group was hot, wet, scratched and exhausted. She turned to Tariq's foster father, who'd joined them for the search. 'Rob, you must have a way of tranquillising a horse from a distance? Can't you use a blowpipe or something?'

Blake Wainright was horrified. 'As if Goldie hasn't been through enough. There's no way I'm going to allow him to be sedated.'

'And neither will I,' objected Brian Meek, the man from the insurance company set to lose millions if Gold Rush couldn't be recovered. He was unsuitably attired in a suit and slippery street shoes. He'd already fallen twice and broken the handle off his briefcase. For reasons unknown, he'd insisted on bringing it.

'Well, the horse can't stay on the moors for much longer,' Calvin Redfern curtly informed him. 'He'll be snatched again or end up injuring himself. If you have a better suggestion, I'd be glad to hear it.'

There was a stony silence as the grown-ups looked to each other for answers and found none. Meanwhile, on the horizon, the object of their frustration guzzled grass contentedly.

'None of this would be happening if his groom was here,' lamented Blake Wainright. 'Ryan Carter, his name is. He's the boy who takes care of Goldie. Been with him since the horse was born. They're inseparable. Unfortunately, he risked his life to stop the thieves stealing Goldie and they put him in the hospital. Looked like an Egyptian mummy when I left, bandages and splints all over the place. It's been a double disaster because Ryan also takes care of Noble Warrior, Goldie's first-born son, who's set to run in the Kentucky Derby in a few weeks' time. It could cost us the race and a lot more. Horses are real sensitive that way. They run best for the people they trust.'

'Tariq could do it,' Laura said suddenly.

There were ten astonished faces, including Tariq's.

The American was taken aback. 'Excuse me?'

'What I mean is, if anyone can catch Goldie it's Tariq. He has a way with animals and Goldie already adores him.'

'She's right,' agreed Rob Ashworth. 'If I'm dealing with a nervous or difficult animal in my surgery I always call Tariq. They seem to trust him on sight.'

34

'Can't hurt,' said Wainright, who was beginning to despair of ever being reunited with his $75 million dollar stallion.

Tariq, who was shy and not at all convinced that he had a special talent with animals or anything else, took a bit of persuading but at last he agreed to try.

What happened next would stay in the minds of all who saw it for years to come. After picking his way towards the red stallion through the heather and gorse, Tariq was met by the same response the search party had encountered all day. Goldie wheeled and galloped away. The difference was that the Bengali boy kept his eyes locked on those of the stallion.

The horse began galloping in circles around him, watching Tariq warily. After a while, Tariq moved his gaze to Goldie's shoulder. The effect was instantaneous. The stallion slowed to a walk. Instead of going up to him, Tariq turned from the horse and stood motionless. After some hesitation, Goldie's curiosity got the better of him. He walked up behind Tariq and did something that caused even the insurance man to blink back a tear. He rested his head on the boy's shoulder.

Blake Wainright drew in an uneven breath. 'Not much surprises me these days, but I have to confess to being stunned. That's an old horse whisperer's trick, but rarely have I seen it done so well. Who knew that it would take a theft and a journey to the wildest reaches of Cornwall, England for me to find the one boy in ten million capable of helping Noble Warrior win the Derby.'

35

'You're not paying attention to a word I'm saying,' scolded Mrs Crabtree.

'Am,' said Laura as her neighbour's fuschia-pink tracksuit and blonde curls came back into focus. Mrs Crabtree was in her sixties, but she dyed her hair and still dressed to stop traffic. 'Well, okay, I was briefly distracted but I'm all ears now.'

'What I was *saying* is that something about this stolen racehorse business smells bad to me and if you had a mind to listen to your elders and betters, you'd walk away now.'

'Nothing to walk away from,' Laura assured her, reaching down to rub Skye's downy ears. 'Goldie's safe and sound and within forty-eight hours he'll be on his way back to Kentucky with Mr Wainright. I doubt we'll set eyes on either of them ever again. Of course the horse thieves are still at large, but that's a police matter now. It's none of my business.'

Mrs Crabtree put one hand on her hip and pointed a garden trowel at Laura with the other. 'Thousands would believe you. *I* don't. When you scent a mystery, you're like that husky with a bone. You'll not let go until it's solved. Well, take some advice from a friend . . .'

'It's really not necessary,' said Laura, gathering Skye's lead, 'but tell me if you must.'

'Don't trust anyone you meet or believe anything you see.'

~ 6 ~

LAURA WAS NOT afraid of flying, but the journey from Charlotte, North Carolina to Lexington, Kentucky tested her nerve. Ten minutes after take-off, the rain shower forecast by air traffic controllers turned into a violent storm. The flight attendant rushed to stow the drinks trolley and issued stern warnings about seatbelts. Almost immediately gale force winds began tossing the little plane around the skies as if it were made of paper. Black raindrops streamed down the windows. Beyond them, the swollen clouds were purple and the late afternoon sky as dark as night.

'Be careful what you wish for . . .'

In the short space of time she had been living with her uncle, Laura had had frequent cause to remember the warning given to her by Matron at the Sylvan Meadows Children's Home, but never once had she wanted to change her new, adrenalin-filled life. Not until this minute at any rate. Now, not even the prospect of spending ten days with her best friend on a Kentucky horse farm, watching some of the most glorious thoroughbreds in racing prepare for the Derby, was of any comfort, especially since it was by no means guaranteed that they'd reach Lexington at all. Not unscathed, at any rate. The sixteen-seater plane was bucking like a furious bronco. Laura wondered how much more it could take. In films, light aircraft seemed to have a nasty habit of disintegrating in storms and going down in flames. She hoped very much that this particular one was sturdier than it appeared.

She glanced at Tariq. He was frightened too, she could tell, but unlike a couple of their fellow passengers, including an unseen woman further up the aisle who was sobbing hysterically, he was doing his best not to show it. He turned from the diamond droplets that splattered the window and saw Laura looking at him. Smiling, he reached for her hand. She squeezed back gratefully.

'Can you believe we're here?' There was real excitement in his voice and she realised that being flung about in mid-air like a leaf in a hurricane hadn't dampened his enthusiasm for the holiday ahead in the least. 'I don't mean on this plane, which is the last place in the world I'd like to be right now, but in the United States? For ten whole days? With *horses!*'

In spite of her fears, Laura couldn't help giggling. Tariq's love of animals was one of the things she liked best about him and his ability to bond with them was the reason for their impromptu trip to Kentucky.

'No,' she told him. 'I can't.'

And she couldn't. It didn't seem real that just two days ago they'd been following Goldie's tracks across the moors, explaining their theory that the horse had escaped rather than been stolen to an incredulous Blake Wainright, Detective Watson and Calvin Redfern, and a disbelieving Vicky.

From the moment Tariq had handed him Goldie's lead rope, Blake Wainright had become obsessed with the notion that he was the only boy on earth who could help Noble Warrior win the Derby. At a dinner to thank Goldie's rescuers, he'd attempted to persuade Calvin Redfern and Rob and Rina Ashworth to pull the children out of school and jump on the next plane to the US to enjoy an all expenses paid trip on his farm in Lexington, Kentucky.

'My wife Christina and I are indebted to you and your kids,' he'd told them. 'Allow us to treat you to the holiday of your dreams. I'm biased, I know, but Fleet Farm is close to heaven in my book. You'll love every minute. Gleaming thoroughbreds everywhere you turn and eighty acres on which Laura and Tariq can ride or play. They'd be great company for my teenage granddaughter, Kit, too. She's not been . . . Well, put it this way, it would do her the world of good to have some young friends around the place. As for the Kentucky Derby itself, it's an unforgettable spectacle.'

Laura and Tariq, who'd overheard the conversation as they helped Rowenna dish up dessert, had started doing little hops of joy. But their celebrations were premature.

'We'd love to take you up on your offer,' Calvin Redfern said, 'but speaking for myself and Laura, it's likely to be next year. I can't take the time off work.'

'Same here,' Rob had agreed. 'I have a busy veterinary practice. I can't just drop everything.'

'And the children have two more weeks of school before the holidays,' Rina pointed out.

But Blake Wainright had refused to take no for an answer. He gave an impassioned speech about how staying on Fleet Farm and seeing close-up what it took to prepare a horse for the biggest race in America would be the experience of a lifetime for the children if they were allowed to come on their own. Calvin Redfern burst out laughing.

'Look, I'm a big believer in travel as education, and I'm sure Rob and Rina feel the same way, but schools have rules and they're not going to break them purely because you feel that nobody but Tariq can help your horse win his race.'

'If the school could be persuaded to let Laura and the boy go, and if my wife homeschooled them for a couple of hours a day while they're there – as she does with Kit – would you consider allowing them to return with me to the US the day after tomorrow?' persisted the American.

'You have no chance of talking the school into it,' Rina assured him. 'The head teacher, Mrs Letchworth, is immoveable on these things.'

'But if she were to say yes, would you let them come?'

Rob smiled. 'I don't see why not. Tariq would be in his element on a horse farm, especially if Laura was with him.'

Calvin Redfern saw no harm in agreeing. As a former Chief Inspector, it had been easy for him to check the Wainrights' background. He'd already established beyond doubt that they were one of the most popular couples in racing, with a reputation for honesty in their business dealings and kindness to their horses. Not that it was likely to matter. Like Rina, he was certain that the school would never allow the children to leave before the end of term.

He'd reckoned without the power of Wainright's chequebook. Next morning, the American had approached the school with a donation generous enough to enable them to build a new library. Hours later Mr Gillbert, Laura's teacher, had informed her in a hushed voice that she and Tariq had been given special permission to travel to Kentucky on a matter of national importance. They'd be leaving within twenty-four hours. He'd then spoiled the surprise by handing them a giant pile of homework to pack in their suitcase.

It had been decided that Blake Wainright would fly with them as far as Charlotte, North Carolina before departing to await the arrival of Gold Rush on a following flight. There were veterinary inspections to be done when the horse entered the US and these could take hours. Wainright would travel the rest of the way to Kentucky in the lorry with Goldie. While it was highly unlikely that the masked raiders would make a further attempt to steal the horse, everyone agreed that it would be safer and more pleasant for the children to complete their journey to Lexington by plane. A flight attendant would take care of them and they'd be met at the airport by Blake's wife, Christina.

Safer and more pleasant? Thirty thousand feet up in a thunderstorm?

Thieves or no thieves, Laura wished that she and Tariq had travelled with Goldie and Blake Wainright in the lorry. The storm was getting worse by the minute.

To take her mind off it, she tried to picture Kit, the Wainwrights' fifteen-year-old granddaughter. Would she be friendly or stuck up? All her life Laura had wished she could have an older sister and when Kit had first been mentioned she'd briefly entertained fantasies that she and the American girl might hang out and have fun together like sisters do. But the realist in Laura knew that was unlikely.

She imagined Kit as pretty and sophisticated – the opposite of Laura who was generally in tatty jeans and an old sweatshirt. She'd practically have been born in the saddle and own a fancy white pony with a long, silky mane. Her bedroom wall would be plastered with rosettes. She'd be grateful that Tariq and Laura had helped rescue Goldie, but she'd find the idea that they could help Noble Warrior win the Derby a joke.

As the plane bounced and swayed in the gale, Laura shook herself mentally. She had to stay positive. 'Just think, Tariq, tomorrow morning when our classmates are sitting down to lessons in St Ives and Mr Gillbert is droning on about algebra, we'll be waking up on a Kentucky horse farm and it's all thanks to you.'

There was a blast of thunder so loud that it sounded as if the plane was about to break in half. Everyone jumped and the woman down the aisle sobbed louder than ever. Tariq gripped Laura's hand. 'Don't thank me until we land in Lexington. We still have to get there in one piece.'

'Oh, we'll get there,' Laura said determinedly. 'We *have* to. Ever since we almost collided with the horsebox, I've had an odd feeling that somehow all of this is meant to be. It's as if nobody but us could have found Gold Rush and nobody but us could have rescued him. As if we were always meant to come here. To America. To Kentucky.'

'As if it were predestined?'

'Yes. As if it were fate.'

Tariq gripped the armrest as the plane dipped and swayed. 'I know exactly what you mean. It's that which makes me wonder . . .'

A fresh wave of adrenalin rippled through Laura. 'Wonder what?'

'What fate has in store for us . . .'

'**WELCOME TO BLUEGRASS** country,' cried Christine Wainright, rushing to greet them as they wandered dazed and trembling into the arrivals hall at Lexington airport. A tall, elegant woman in a navy blue suit, she shook Laura and Tariq's hands very formally before spontaneously giving each of them a hug.

'It doesn't seem right to stand on ceremony when I feel as if I already know you,' she said. 'My husband has spoken so highly of you both that I'm afraid I already consider you friends. We are so deeply in your debt. If you and Mr Redfern hadn't saved Goldie . . . well, it just doesn't bear thinking about. I expect Blake told you, we love that horse like a child. All our horses are like family to us, but Goldie and Noble Warrior – he's our Derby baby – they'll always have a special place in our hearts.'

Mrs Wainright had an accent as slow and melodic as that of her husband and silver-blonde hair swept up into a bun. Her smile was warm and outlined in mulberry. There was no sign of her granddaughter, Kit. She said worriedly: 'Your journey was bearable, I trust? The storm didn't make it too bumpy?'

Laura didn't have the heart to tell her that they'd spent most of the flight fearing for their lives, were nervous wrecks and more than a little queasy. 'It was great,' she lied. 'A bit bumpy but nothing we couldn't handle.'

Tariq mustered a grin. 'No problem at all.'

Christine laughed. 'From what my husband tells me, the pair of you can handle quite a lot. My granddaughter, Kit, is looking forward to meeting you, but she had to stay behind and finish some schoolwork. Now you must be shattered. How about I whisk you home to Fleet Farm?'

It was not until she sank into the springy backseat of the Cadillac that Laura realised how exhausted she was, or how cold. She was relieved when Christine put on the car heater. The drive to the farm passed in a haze. The departing storm had smudged the sky with violet and yellow bruises. It hung low over the parallel lines of the white fences that framed the picture-perfect homes of America's finest racehorses.

'Double fences to keep the stallions in and the mares and foals out or vice versa,' Christine explained.

Tariq had his nose pressed to the window, not wanting to miss a thing. 'Why here?' he asked, as they began to pass farm after farm where sleek, shining bays, chestnuts and greys grazed in emerald-green pastures. Fluffy foals with impossibly long legs experimented with wobbly bursts of speed. 'Why did Kentucky become one of the best places in the world to raise a racehorse?'

'The secret lies in the Kentucky Bluegrass. And before you ask why it isn't blue, it has that name because it has tiny cornflower-blue flowers if it's allowed to grow to full height. Which it rarely is. The reason it's so good for racehorses is that the soil is rich in limestone and calcium. As they eat they take in nutrients that build strong bones and legs of iron.'

'Is that what Noble Warrior has?' Laura wanted to know. 'Legs of iron?'

Christine smiled. 'That and his sire's big heart. Like Goldie, he'll give you everything he has and then he'll reach inside and find something more. He's a sweetheart too, though people who see him race find that hard to believe. On the track he's all fire and fury. Off it, he's as soppy and loveable as a Labrador. But he's nervy. That's the reason Blake was so keen to bring you over, Tariq. If Warrior's routine is upset, he's like a scared little boy. Since Ryan's been in hospital, Warrior has been out of sorts and running poorly in training. My husband is hoping that you'll be able to work your magic and have him racing at full strength by the Derby.'

There was a pause as she slowed the car, turned and stopped in front of high iron gates. Overhead a scrolling sign announced Fleet Farm. The gates purred open. Beyond them was a paved driveway lined with white fences.

Laura had noticed that what made the farms unique were their colourful painted barns. Fleet had two. The mares' and foals' barn was cream with a green roof and red shutters. The stallion barn, a black one trimmed with white shutters and a red bell tower, stood proudly on a hill against the stormy sky. As they drew nearer, a young man in a baseball cap emerged from it and began hosing down a bay horse. Christine waved and called to him, but his only response was to touch the brim of his hat. Face sullen, he resumed what he was doing. When Laura glanced back, he was watching them go. His body language reminded her of a hostile terrier.

'Was that one of the grooms?' she asked.

Christine shook her head. 'That's Ken, Noble Warrior's exercise rider. He's helping out with a couple of the horses while Ryan is in hospital. They're best friends, you see. Ken took it very hard when the horsebox was hijacked and Ryan and the driver, Jason, were attacked. Blames himself. He was supposed to have gone with them on what was meant to be a routine outing to take Goldie to the Equine Hospital for a checkup. Instead he slipped off to watch a football game. When Ryan was beaten half to death and Goldie stolen, he was devastated.'

Her mouth tightened. 'He can be a bit moody sometimes, Ken. Don't take anything he says to heart. Underneath it all he's a good boy – one of our best.'

The Cadillac glided over the hill and came to a halt in a storm-darkened yard ablaze with pink, purple and yellow rhododendrons and azaleas. Towering over them was a white mansion flanked by the largest oak trees the children had ever seen. The front door was at least twice as tall as that at number 28 Ocean View Terrace and had a stained glass image of the winged horse Pegasus inset into the heavy wood. White pillars lent a Colonial air to the grey-tiled porch.

Laura climbed stiffly out of the car and looked up at the house. 'It's beautiful,' she said in awe. 'I think it's the most lovely place I've ever seen.'

For an instant Christina's eyes seemed to sparkle with tears, but they were gone in blink. 'I feel the same way. That's what makes it so hard that . . . that we have to . . . Let's put it this way: whether or not we get to keep Fleet Farm has a lot to do with how Noble Warrior performs in the Derby.'

She turned to Tariq, who was lifting the luggage from the boot of the car. 'My husband was rather vague on your background, my dear. How did you become such an expert on horses at such a young age?'

The Bengali boy set the suitcase down and smiled. 'I'm not.'

Christina paled beneath her tan, but she said brightly. 'You're being modest, I assume. Laura, is he always so self-effacing? Presumably, Tariq, you've had quite a bit of experience grooming them, riding them or healing them? Blake seemed to feel that you were England's answer to the horse whisperer.'

Tariq regarded her with clear amber eyes. 'I've learned a little about horses in the last few months while I've been living with my foster father – he's a vet, but I've never ridden a horse and Goldie is the first I've ever touched. I'm definitely not a horse, dog or any other kind of whisperer. Animals seem to like me, that's all.'

'They *like* you?' All of a sudden Christine looked every day of her sixty-eight years. 'How about you, Laura? Please tell me that you're a great rider or have spent hundreds of hours watching racing or hanging out at your local stables. Please tell me that you at least are an accomplished horsewoman?'

'I'm not,' admitted Laura, hating to disappoint her. In her short acquaintance with Mrs Wainright, she'd grown to like the woman as much as she did her husband. 'I know even less about horses than Tariq does, and I've never in my life been riding. The only thing I'm quite good at is solving mysteries and finding clues. Your husband seemed to think that might be quite useful around here.'

'Mysteries? Clues? Dear God, it sounds like something out of a detective novel.' Christine leaned on a column for support. 'Just when I thought things couldn't get any worse, my husband has put the future of Fleet Farm into the hands of two youngsters who barely know one end of a horse from another.'

~ 8 ~

LAURA AWOKE WITH a start thinking she was in her bed at number 28 Ocean View Terrace. The room was so dark that she panicked and reached for Skye. Usually he slept at the foot of her mattress, taking up more than his fair share of space. When she recalled that she was in Kentucky, far from her husky and the uncle she adored, she felt a pang so sharp it brought tears to her eyes.

Lightning shivered across the room, briefly illuminating the oak corners of the four-poster bed, the rocking chair and assorted Kentucky Derby memorabilia. On the wall opposite a photograph showed the beaming Wainrights posing with Gold Rush after his Derby win. The famous garland – four hundred red roses sewn onto green silk – adorned his powerful chestnut neck. The garland was the reason that the race was nicknamed the 'Run for the Roses'.

Above the dresser was a framed newspaper article about Goldie's victory, headlined: "**KENTUCKY THRILLER: Gold Rush Proves his Worth in Derby Triumph**.' In the accompanying grainy photo, the red stallion was at full stretch, every sinew straining. All four hooves were off the ground and he looked as if he were flying. The reporter described the race as the 'most exciting two minutes in sport'.

The rain pitter-pattered against the window. Laura groped for her watch on the bedside table. It wasn't there and she didn't have the energy to hunt for it, nor did she want to put on the light. Was it midnight? Two a.m.? Three-thirty? She hadn't the faintest.

She wondered if Tariq, sleeping in the adjoining room, was awake, and, if not, whether he'd mind if she disturbed him and said that she was homesick and wanted a chat. She doubted it. Despite his horrific background in a Bangladesh quarry, a dusty hell that had led to the deaths of his mum and dad, Tariq was the most easygoing and kind-hearted boy she knew.

She was poised to knock on his door when she heard a car engine. Tiptoeing to the window in her pyjamas, she peered out into the rainy dark. It was Goldie and Blake Wainright arriving home after their long journey from North Carolina. Her bedroom was on the second floor and she had an unrestricted, if blurry, view of the barn and the lorry. Three black-cloaked figures were milling around in the white triangle of headlights. The distance and slanting rain made it impossible for Laura to make out their faces and their hoods disguised them further.

One of the men lowered the ramp of the lorry and another untied the horse. As the stallion stepped carefully down the slope, the light fell on his chestnut hide. He disappeared into the barn with the cloaked figures. Moments later, the lorry started up and rumbled away down the drive.

The tallest of the three men emerged from the barn and strode up the hill towards the house. Laura caught a glimpse of Blake Wainright's snowy hair beneath his hood and was glad that he and his horse were safely home.

A wave of tiredness came over her and she returned to bed. Sinking into the mattress was like being swallowed by a cloud. Almost before her head touched the pillow, she was unconscious again.

Hours or maybe minutes later she woke again. Her eyes opened to the lightning's ghostly flicker. It was still pitch dark. She reached for Skye and felt a painful wrench as she remembered that she was in Kentucky, far from home. She wondered what time it was and reached for her watch. It was only then that she recalled that she'd already been through this exact routine. She'd been awake earlier in the night and seen Goldie and Blake Wainright return.

Rain was falling softly. Over its musical tinkle she caught the faint rumble of an engine. Jumping out of bed, she ran to the window. A lorry was backing up to the barn. Three hooded, black-cloaked figures were fussing around it. They lowered the ramp. One climbed into the lorry and emerged leading a chestnut horse.

Laura was confused. Had she or hadn't she seen Goldie being unloaded earlier that night? Had she dreamed it, or was she dreaming now?

She pinched herself hard. No, she was definitely awake. Since it was unlikely that the Wainrights were having two chestnut horses delivered in the dead of night, that could only mean she'd dreamed Goldie's arrival earlier. How weird that the dream had been so accurate – a virtual premonition. It wasn't hard to believe that her imagination could conjure up the red stallion, given the time she'd spent with him in Cornwall, but how could she have known that the men would be wearing black cloaks? The lorry too was identical.

The men disappeared into the barn. Then something strange happened. The chestnut horse was led back out of the barn and loaded onto the lorry. The ramp was raised, the red brake lights pulsed and the lorry drove quietly away.

Laura stared out at the barn. Aside from the soft hiss of rain, all was silent and still. She felt dizzy with tiredness. What had just happened? Why had Mr Wainwright brought Goldie home only to send him away again? Or was the outgoing chestnut another horse altogether? If so, what did that mean? Had she dreamed some of it or none of it? How much time had passed between delivery and departure?

Laura returned to the cloud bed, head spinning. Sleep hovered. She gave up trying to keep her eyelids from drooping and surrendered to the mattress's snug embrace.

There was a faint sound. Tariq's slim shadow was at the door. 'Laura, are you awake?'

Laura sat bolt upright. It suddenly occurred to her that what she'd witnessed must have been a theft. Why else would the hooded figures have driven off with a chestnut stallion? She hadn't seen the blaze on the horse's face so she couldn't positively identify him as Gold Rush, but they'd definitely been the same colour, the russet hue of leaves at the height of autumn.

'Tariq, did you see the lorry that just drove away?'

He perched on the edge of the bed. His voice was husky with tiredness. 'What lorry? Is that what woke me? I thought it was thunder.'

Quickly Laura told him what had happened. But even as she attempted to explain what she'd seen, she could hear how ridiculous it sounded. A horse that may or may not have been Goldie had arrived at an indeterminate time in the night. Some while later another horse or perhaps the same one had been taken away again. A robbery might have taken place, or Laura might simply have been dreaming.

Tariq looked doubtful. 'Is there any part of the story you're absolutely sure about?'

Laura thought about it. 'I definitely saw Mr Wainright walking towards the house after the first horse had been delivered, and I definitely saw the second horse, or the same horse, being taken away again. I think I did anyway.'

'But you're not a hundred per cent convinced that you didn't imagine part of it?'

Laura was indignant. 'I was wide awake when the

second horse was driven away. You know I was because I sat up as soon as you came in.'

'No, you didn't. I spoke to you three times before you answered.'

Laura slumped back into the pillows. 'You don't believe me.'

He tugged at her pyjama sleeve. 'I do believe you. I do. It's just that . . . well, you're not certain what happened either.'

The outline of his face had grown clearer. Through the crack in the curtains, dawn was approaching. Outside the window, a cheerful bird was celebrating the end of a long, wet night.

'What if everything I saw was real?' Laura said. 'Goldie arrived and the lorry left, then later the same lorry or an identical one returned with another chestnut horse. Shortly afterwards, it drove off carrying a chestnut that might have been Goldie or might not. What would that mean?'

'It probably means you're right – Goldie or one of the other stallions has been stolen.'

Laura sat up again. 'So what do we do about it?'

But she already knew what they had to do. Beside the bed was a red panic button. Christine had pointed it out when she'd shown her and Tariq to their rooms, explaining in great detail that it was only to be used in the most extreme emergency since it not only woke up the household and brought Fleet Farm's security manager running, it also roused the local police.

With a nervous glance at Tariq, she reached out a hand and pressed it.

'TELL ME AGAIN why you thought Goldie had been kidnapped?'

Laura knew that Blake Wainright was being as understanding as could be expected under the circumstances, especially since he'd only had two hours sleep and was exhausted after his epic journey across the Atlantic. All the same she wanted to crawl under the breakfast table and hide. For the twentieth time that morning she began a halting account of the night's events.

Christine, who felt sorry for her, said encouragingly: 'Blake arrived home with Goldie at about two-fifteen a.m., so you definitely witnessed that. I'm afraid you must have dreamed the rest. You've had quite an exciting time of it recently, what with rescuing a champion racehorse twice and flying halfway round the world. It's hardly surprising if some things get scrambled in sleep.'

She smiled. 'Don't give it another thought. Now why don't you have one of Anita's famous waffles? You've hardly eaten a thing.'

The sun was spilling in through the French doors, forming droplets of gold on the starched white tablecloth, and the scent of jasmine mingled with the aromas of coffee and maple syrup. The events of the night seemed more surreal than ever. Laura nibbled miserably at one of the waffles conjured up by the Wainrights' Hispanic cook, Anita. It was indeed delicious, but after a couple of bites she laid down her knife and fork. Her stomach was in knots. She and Tariq had been in Kentucky for a matter of hours. How could everything have gone so wrong?

Pushing the panic button had, as expected, caused instant pandemonium. First, Christine and Blake came tearing into the room in their dressing gowns, hair awry. In their wake was what resembled a slim, pale boy wearing blue-spotted pyjamas. It was only when the lights blazed that Laura saw that the 'boy' was in fact a teenage girl with short, mousy hair that stuck out in every direction. In the chaos, no one remembered that Laura and Tariq had not yet been introduced to Kit, the Wainrights' elusive granddaughter. She hadn't been at dinner and there had been no explanations as to her whereabouts.

Throughout the drama, and there had been plenty of it, Kit had hung back and never once uttered a word.

Not even when the cops had come blasting up the drive, blue lights twirling. Plump with doughnuts and bristling with weaponry, they'd rushed about barking orders and directing a machine-gun volley of questions at Laura and Tariq. At one point, Laura had been quite sure that she was about to be arrested.

The most intimidating man on the scene by far, however, had been Fleet Farm's head of security, Garth Longbrook, a former commando in the US Navy. He was balding, super fit and not amused at being dragged from his bed less than two hours after he'd climbed into it.

'Save me from amateur detectives,' he'd said sarcastically in a voice loud enough for Laura to hear after he'd searched the barn and found all eight stallions, including Goldie, standing happily in their stalls. Not so much as a wisp of hay was out of place. Noble Warrior had been a little agitated, but Garth Longbrook claimed that this was to only to be expected given the number of strangers invading the barn.

'What time did you see this *supposed* second lorry?' he'd demanded of Laura, even though she'd already stated five or six times that she had no idea. She bitterly regretted that she hadn't summoned up the energy to turn on the light and find a clock. She'd eventually located her watch under the bed.

'If only I'd made the effort to get it, I'd know for certain whether there was another lorry or if it was a dream after all,' she'd whispered to Tariq.

Not that she'd said that to Garth Longbrook. When she'd asked if there was CCTV footage of the barn that could be checked, he'd regarded her with barely concealed dislike before marching off, muttering to himself, to do just that. Thirty minutes later, he'd triumphantly led Laura, Tariq and Blake Wainright into his office and scrolled through the black and white footage of the night to demonstrate that there was no evidence of any vehicle, apart from the one that had brought Goldie and Blake Wainright, loading or offloading a chestnut horse in the dead of night.

The more people tried to prove to Laura that she was mistaken, the more convinced she became that she was right. She *had* seen something. Something *had* happened. The only question was what.

'How often does the camera scan the barn?' she'd asked as they gathered in Garth's office, a meticulously ordered space in the office building adjacent to the main house.

He'd swivelled in his chair and regarded her with a look that could have fossilised a tree. 'Every ten minutes.'

'So in theory the lorry could have come and gone in that time?'

Out of the corner of her eye, Laura noticed Kit glance up sharply. A small smile seemed to play around her mouth, but it was gone before Laura could be sure.

'It's possible but not probable, isn't that right, Garth?' said Blake Wainright. 'The men in the lorry would have had to know exactly when each ten-minute cycle started and stopped, and even then it would have been a challenge for them to enter the farm through a locked and alarmed gate, offload one horse and reload a different horse in such a short time. That would suggest that it was an inside job, which I refuse to accept.'

His head of security did not bother to disguise the impatience in his voice. 'With respect, sir, might I remind you that NO crime has been committed. Nothing has been taken. The horses are safely in their stalls. There *was* no second lorry.'

Blake Wainright gave a deep chuckle, lightening the mood. 'Quite right, Garth, no crime has been committed. However, I'm grateful to Laura for alerting us when she thought one had been. Better safe than sorry is my motto. Now I don't know about anyone else but I'm starving. Who wants breakfast?'

The morning sun had chased away the storm's gloom, but it failed to lift Laura's mood. Tariq kept trying to catch her eye and pull funny faces to make her laugh, but it didn't work. Part of her felt embarrassed and guilty for waking up the whole household and creating so much chaos. The other half was determined to find out the truth about what had happened.

She looked up to find the silent Kit watching her. The girl glanced away quickly, letting her fringe flop over her eyes like a curtain. She was dressed like a cowboy, in a blue-checked flannel shirt, jeans and worn range-rider boots. 'May I be excused, Grandma?' she said.

Christine smiled at her, but the smile, Laura thought, contained a warning. 'You may be excused, honey, but only from the table. Your grandfather and I have some business to attend to. I'd very much appreciate it if you could show Laura and Tariq around Fleet Farm. I'm sure they'd love to say hello to Goldie and meet Noble Warrior.'

Kit scowled. 'Can't Ken do it? I'm not a babysitter. I want to finish my book.'

Laura was shocked by the girl's rudeness. She said quickly: 'I'm sure Tariq and I can find our own way around the farm.'

Christine continued as if she hadn't spoken. 'Kit, sweetie, you'll have plenty of time to read your book later and Ken is very busy. It's wonderful for you to have some youngsters to hang out with for a change rather than us old folk. I hope you'll make the most of it.'

The look on Kit's face said she'd rather drink a toad smoothie than hang out with Laura and Tariq, but she mumbled, 'Yes, Grandma.'

Her grandfather reached out a large tanned hand and squeezed her shoulder. His eyes crinkled at the corners. 'Hey Possum, don't forget that we owe Laura and Tariq a big debt of gratitude for saving Goldie. They'll always be heroes in my eyes. A few hours of lost sleep is not going to change that.'

Kit murmured obediently, 'Yes, Gramps,' and was out of the door before he could say anything else.

Blake gave Laura and Tariq an apologetic smile and lifted his hands. 'Girls will be girls,' he said lightly, but Laura thought he looked sad.

They'd caught up with Kit and were halfway down the garden when the American girl stopped abruptly. She had the same denim blue eyes as her grandfather, but without the twinkle that made his so appealing.

'Let's be clear,' she snapped, 'I'm not the one who owes you anything. I don't care about stupid Goldie. He could have stayed kidnapped for all I care. If it weren't that Grandma and Gramps would be broken-hearted, I wouldn't care if a hundred thieves stole every one of our horses. I hate them. All they do is cause trouble. And you're not heroes to me. You're just a couple of strangers who are going to get in the way of my reading and guitar playing. Books and music are the only friends I want. The sooner you go back to where you came from, the better.'

Laura and Tariq stared at her in open-mouthed disbelief, but it turned out that she wasn't finished.

'Oh, and by the way the idea that some boy who doesn't know the first thing about horses can help Noble Warrior win the Derby is the most idiotic thing I've ever heard.'

Tariq recovered first. 'First, we would never in a million years think of ourselves as heroes. Lots of people helped rescue Goldie. We just happened to be two of them. Secondly, we love animals – especially horses and dogs – so *we're* glad that Goldie's safe even if you're not. As to whether or not I can help Noble Warrior win the Derby, I agree that it's a pretty crazy idea. After last night, your grandfather probably does too. But Laura and I like Mr and Mrs Wainright a lot and we're honoured that they've invited us to their beautiful farm. If we can help them with Noble Warrior, even in a small way, we're going to do our best.'

Now it was Kit's turn to look shocked. 'Umm, look, I didn't mean . . .' Her voice tailed away.

Laura was bristling with indignation. She could not believe that this odd girl with the sticking up hair and tomboy clothes had just told them to their faces that the sooner they left, the better she'd like it.

She lifted her chin and stared Kit in the eye. 'I agree with Tariq. We think your Grandma and Gramps are wonderful and we're going to do what we can to help them, whether you think that's idiotic or not. Oh, and you don't have to worry about us getting in the way of your reading. Tariq and I have each other. We don't need another friend.'

Before Kit could respond, Anita called: 'Miss Laura! Miss Laura, hurry. Your uncle is on the phone. He say they catch 'um. They catch the wicked men who stole Goldie.'

~ 10 ~

LAURA TOOK THE call in the airy living room beneath an immense oil painting of a jockey holding the reins of a bay stallion. It was so nice to hear her uncle's kind, calm voice and Skye barking in the background that Laura felt emotional again, but she forgot her own troubles as soon as she heard Calvin Redfern's news.

'Detective Watson has just called,' he told her. 'I thought you'd like to know that he's made two arrests in the Goldie case – a father and his twenty-five-year-old son. They run an international horse transportation business, which made it relatively easy for them to get the stallion across the Atlantic with forged paperwork.'

64

'So the Straight A gang weren't involved?' was Laura's first question.

Her uncle laughed. 'You sound almost disappointed. No, the Straight A's were not involved. As far as the police can tell, the two men acted alone. Their family business was about to go bankrupt and they thought that kidnapping a multi-million dollar racehorse and sending ransom notes would be the quickest way to make themselves a small fortune. They weren't planning to take the horse out of America, but when the ransom wasn't paid and it looked as if the police were hot on their trail, they panicked and put him on a flight to the UK. They were on their way to deliver him to a potential buyer when a deer leapt out in front of them and the horsebox overturned. Thinking the stallion was dead, they abandoned him.'

'Oh,' Laura said, feeling strangely dissatisfied. She should have been happy that the mystery of Goldie's abduction had been solved and the thieves were behind bars, but she wasn't. The events of the past few hours haunted her.

'That means the case is now closed, Laura,' her uncle was saying firmly. 'No more investigating. Blake Wainright has just told me what happened at Fleet Farm last night. You did the right thing to raise the alarm when you thought a theft had taken place, but it's obvious that it's greatly inconvenienced everyone concerned. From this moment on, you and Tariq are to remember that you're in Kentucky on holiday. You're forbidden to poke your nose into other people's business. No looking for mysteries where there are none, or seeing criminals where there are only decent men and women trying to do their jobs.'

'Yes, Uncle Calvin.'

'Don't say yes if you don't mean it.'

'Yes, Uncle Calvin. I mean, no, Uncle Calvin. Of course, Uncle Calvin.'

He sighed. 'It's at times such as this that I wish you and I weren't quite so alike. Oh, well, I guess I'll have to trust you. Now how about saying hello to Skye.'

When Laura went outside, Tariq and Kit were standing a couple of metres apart and in silence. The American girl was wearing a scowl. She stalked off towards the stallion barn without a word. Ignoring her, Laura relayed the news about the capture of Goldie's kidnappers to Tariq. Kit pretended she couldn't care less, but as soon as Laura had finished she turned and said: 'Thank goodness for that. Now everyone will stop going on and on about Goldie until I could scream, and life can get back to normal around here.'

They were almost at the barn when Laura noticed sunlight glinting from a metallic object close to where the lorries had parked the previous night. Unnoticed by the others, she bent down and picked it up. It was a piece of something silver. What remained resembled a lopsided tick or part of a letter of the alphabet – the top of an A or the fork of a V or Y. Laura popped it into her pocket. In all probability it was nothing, but one never knew. The most unlikely things could turn out to be clues.

Recalling her promise to her uncle, she felt guilty. Then she remembered that, according to all the grown-ups there *was* no mystery about the previous night. 'NO crime has been committed,' Garth Longbrook had declared. If that were true, there would be no harm whatsoever in taking a closer look at what went on behind the scenes at Fleet Farm. If there were no illegal goings on, a little poking around could hardly be considered an investigation. There was nothing wrong with healthy curiosity.

Inside the light, airy barn were a dozen beautifully clean stables. Four were empty, but the sculpted heads of some of America's finest thoroughbreds hung over the rest. They turned dark, interested eyes as the children approached. Kit introduced each one, but stood as far from them as possible. While Laura and Tariq stroked their velvet muzzles and went into raptures about their sleek, muscled forms, she hung back, looking strangely wistful.

Goldie was in the eighth stable. He remembered them at once and whickered with pleasure. Incredibly, he looked no worse for wear for his ordeal.

'If he has jet lag, he's hiding it well,' joked Tariq.

Ken emerged from the office beside the stable, looking even surlier that he had the previous day. When he saw Kit his eyebrows rose slightly, but he made no comment.

'This is Laura and Tariq,' Kit told him. 'They want to meet Noble Warrior. Gramps says that, unless Ryan gets out of hospital sooner than expected, Tariq is to be Warrior's groom between now and the Derby.'

Ken ignored Laura but gave the Bengali boy a slightly contemptuous look. 'Does he now? Had much experience grooming champion racehorses, kid?'

'No,' admitted Tariq, feeling foolish. 'But I'm a hard worker and a quick learner.'

Ken shrugged. 'In that case, you can start at once.'

'Great,' said Kit. 'I'll leave you to it.' Before anyone could object, she was gone.

Ken pushed open the office door, revealing a small, homely space that had the aroma of fresh coffee. A black and white cat was curled up in the sunshine on the windowsill. Racing photographs papered the walls. A young man with tangled blonde hair that hung almost to his shoulders was sitting at the table juggling rainbow-coloured skittles. A foreign language newspaper was spread out beside him.

'Don't let Mitch Raydon catch you doing that,' warned Ken.

The young man bounced to his feet with a cheeky grin. 'I am doing what?'

Laura blinked. The skittles had gone.

He came forward with his hand outstretched. 'My name is Ivan and I hear already that you are Miss Laura and Mr Tariq. We have you to sank many times for finding Goldie for us. We owe you. Anysing you need while you are here, ask Ivan.' He winked at Laura. 'If you ask Ken, don't hold your breath.'

'Very funny,' said Ken with a scowl. 'That's rich coming from the most work-shy man on the farm. And you wonder why Mitch gives you such a hard time. Now, where is that spare jacket? I left it hanging over the back of a chair.'

'Perhaps Mitch put it in locker. He's neat freak – zat's what zey say in your country, is it not?' Ivan pulled open a few lockers and drawers. When he discovered it, he presented it to Tariq with a flourish. 'Zis is very big but you can push up the sleeves, I sink.'

The jacket had the words 'FLEET FARM' and a galloping horse sketched in white on the back. Laura was as sure as she could be that the men in both lorries had worn cloaks with the identical logo. She'd been some distance away and looking down on the scene through a blur of rain, but she recognised the shape.

The jacket almost swamped Tariq, but he put it on with a smile and Ivan rolled up the sleeves for him.

'Don't you have work to do, Ivan?' demanded Ken.

The young man gave a mock salute. 'Aye, aye, captain.' He flashed the children another grin. 'Remember what I tell you. Anysing you need, ask for Ivan.' Then he was gone.

Ken escorted them to the last stable in the row. Noble Warrior was standing in the rear of the stable with his ears back, resting one foot. Christine had described him as a sweetheart, but to Laura he looked bored and out of sorts.

'You'll notice that he's much smaller than Goldie, his sire,' Ken told them. 'Tiny but perfectly formed. That's because he's a twin – something almost unheard of in racing. He has an identical brother named Valiant, who belongs to Nathan Perry, owner of the farm next door. When they're standing still, the only person who can tell them apart is Ryan. But there's a big difference in their speed. Valiant is an okay horse, but Warrior is dynamite. We call him the Pocket Rocket.'

Laura noticed that while he was talking about the horses that were his passion, Ken's face came alive and his eyes sparkled with enthusiasm. When he stopped, his sullen look returned. He unbolted the stable door and nodded at Tariq. 'You think you can help Warrior win the Kentucky Derby? Here he is. Introduce yourself to him.'

With an anxious glance at Laura, Tariq walked into the stable. Laura, who was annoyed with Ken for testing her friend – and she had no doubt that that's what this was, a test – followed him in.

Noble Warrior snorted uneasily and showed the whites of his eyes. Tariq hesitated.

'You're not afraid, are you?' jeered Ken. 'That wouldn't be a good start. A groom who's afraid of horses.'

'No, I'm not. But I'm worried that something is bothering him.'

'Most racehorses are like human athletes,' Ken told him. 'They're pampered and indulged and that tends to make them moody. You need to be able to handle that. But you don't need to fret about Warrior. He's a pussy cat.'

Tariq took a step further and Noble Warrior's chestnut ears pinned flat against his head. Again the boy hesitated. Ken made another jibe. It was on the tip of Laura's tongue to say, 'Something's wrong. I don't think we should be in here,' when the horse exploded.

With a squeal of fury, he reared, striking out with his hooves. Tariq and Laura barely had time to leap for the stable door before he came after them, teeth bared. Laura felt the rush of air as his jaws snapped shut just millimeters from her arm. He wheeled and tried to kick

Tariq. Ken grabbed the boy and wrenched the stable door closed in the nick of time. The horse's hooves clattered against it. Noble Warrior let out another scream of rage.

'What the heck is going on here?' demanded Blake Wainright. Kit was beside him, eyes wide with terror, and behind her was a short, wiry man with a leathery brown face and glittery black eyes. Laura wondered if he was the trainer, Mitch Raydon. Blake Wainright advanced on Ken. 'If Warrior is injured and can't run in the Derby, we're finished. Do you understand that? Finished.'

Ken looked shaken himself. 'I'm so sorry, sir. I don't know what to say. As soon as Tariq and Laura entered the stable, Warrior went berserk. He seemed to be trying to kill them.'

Mitch Raydon moved nearer. 'Obviously, this means that the boy can't be his groom. If Ken hasn't the time, I'll get Ivan to do it.'

'It means nothing of the kind,' Blake Wainright responded irritably. 'Warrior must have got some sort of fright, that's all. Now Tariq, you and I will go into the stable together. Take that silly jacket off. It's much too large for you and it'll simply get in your way if you're working with him. Christine is going to order some Fleet Farm clothing for you and Laura. You'll be much more comfortable in something your own size. Now I know you've had a fright, but trust me when I say that Noble Warrior is as gentle as a kitten. Let me introduce you to him.'

Tariq handed the jacket to Laura and their eyes met. She could see that he wasn't looking forward to another encounter with the stallion.

Blake opened the stable door. 'All you have to do is approach him with the same calm confidence you had when you were dealing with Goldie.'

The boy stepped into the stall, talking all the time in a low, calm voice. The horse was sweating and trembling but he made no move to attack. Tariq crept forward until he was near enough to touch the horse. Cautiously, he put a hand on the stallion's neck. Noble Warrior tensed. He turned his head, snorting with fear. His muzzle touched Tariq's chest. Tariq stroked his graceful head with kind hands. Warrior began to relax. At length, he gave a great shuddering sigh and all the tension left his body.

The tautness drained from Blake Wainright's body too. He chuckled. 'There you go! What did I tell you? They're made for each other.'

For the next half hour, Ken gave Tariq an advanced grooming lesson under Blake's watchful eye. Kit had disappeared again and Mitch had excused himself to supervise the arrival of a new mare. Leaning over the stable door, Laura felt immensely proud of her friend. Few boys would have had the courage to return to the stable after what had happened, but he'd done so without hesitation.

At the same time, she couldn't help wondering about the transformation in the stallion. He'd changed from savage mustang to angel in seconds for no obvious reason. What had set him off? The only thing Tariq had done differently was to remove the jacket.

Blake, Tariq and Ken were absorbed with the horse. Laura moved out of view. She studied the jacket. It looked new and clean. Ken had put on one just like it and Noble

Warrior hadn't batted an ear. On impulse, she lifted it to her nose and almost gagged. The right sleeve smelled strongly of – of what?

Laura tried to work it out. It reminded her of something. She wracked her brains. Then, it came to her. It was reminiscent of the big cat enclosure at the zoo near Sylvan Meadows. A foster family had taken her there when she was nine. She'd stood outside the lion cage, breathing in their wild smell, a smell she was sure would be natural and even wonderful on the plains of Africa but which was rancid and overpowering in the confined space. To Laura, who'd wept at the sight of the forlorn lions shivering in the British winter, it was the smell of unhappiness.

But how could such a smell get onto a supposedly clean jacket at a horse farm in Kentucky? More importantly, why?

Instinctively, horses are petrified of big cats, their main predator in ancient times. If someone had deliberately daubed the scent of a lion or something similar on the jacket, there could be only one explanation, that he or she had wanted to terrify a horse and, presumably, the wearer. But which horse and who was the intended victim? The jacket had apparently been a random one found in a locker. Was it too much of a leap to think that it was always intended for Tariq and meant to scare him so much that he'd refuse to help Noble Warrior?

Laura wondered if she could sneak the jacket up to her room and keep it in a safe place until an opportunity arose to examine it more closely, but before she could think of how to conceal it Ken emerged from the stable. 'You done with that?' he asked grouchily and practically snatched the jacket away.

She couldn't protest without causing a scene. Watching him disappear into the office, a frown creased Laura's brow. She'd been at Fleet Farm for less than twenty-four hours but one thing was crystal clear. There were many more questions than answers.

11

'**I WOULDN'T TAKE** them riding for all the tea in China,' declared Kit.

Outside the breakfast room, Laura and Tariq exchanged glances. It didn't take a rocket scientist to guess who she was talking about. The previous night, she'd stayed completely silent at dinner when Blake was telling his wife about the visitors' dramatic meeting with Noble Warrior. Recalling the girl's stricken face and sudden exit from the barn, it had occurred to Laura then that there might be more to her behaviour than met the eye.

'*I wouldn't care if a hundred thieves stole every one of our* horses,' she'd ranted earlier in the day. *'I hate them. All they do is cause trouble.'*

What trouble, Laura wondered. Was it something to do with the finances of the farm? And why did the girl detest horses so much? Christine had told them that Kit's parents were divorced. Her mum was a busy professional who spent much of her time travelling, and Kit rarely saw her father. She'd been all but brought up by the grandparents she adored. To Laura, that made it more curious still that Kit hadn't inherited their love of horses. She could hardly bear to touch them.

Kit showed no sign of embarrassment when they entered the dining room, although she must have known they'd overheard her.

Christine, however, looked mortified. 'Come in, come in,' she said, mustering an over-bright smile. 'I hope you slept well. Help yourself to a couple of Anita's fluffy pecan pancakes. There's farm butter, cream and strawberries to go on top, and maple syrup in the jug.'

They were tucking into mountainous heaps of syrupy pancakes when she brought up the subject of riding again. 'I was just saying to Kit that I'd like her to take you both horseback riding this morning. If that's something you'd enjoy, that is.'

Kit's mouth set in a mutinous line.

With a pleading glance at her, Christine continued: 'Kit prefers not to ride herself, but I was about to suggest that she escort you on her bicycle. Would that be okay with everyone?'

Before any of the children could agree or disagree, she

said: 'Good, then that's settled. Kit will meet you both at the mares' and foals' barn, which is where we keep our working horses, at ten a.m. Your horses will be saddled and waiting, and she'll be ready with her bike. Now, can I interest anyone in some coffee?'

U

'My wife says it is a crying shame,' said Roberto, Anita's husband, whose job it was to take care of the mares, foals and working horses. He tightened the girth on Laura's horse, a pretty palomino.

Laura followed his gaze and saw Kit cycling slowly up from the house. She dismounted and began examining a tyre as if inspecting it for a puncture.

'What's a crying shame?' asked Tariq, leading his own pony, a brown and white paint horse, in their direction. He'd been up since the crack of dawn taking care of Noble Warrior, but he was positively glowing. Nothing made him happier than being around animals.

Roberto handed the palomino's reins to Laura. 'Is it not a shame when the best young horsewoman in Kentucky choose two wheels over a horse?'

Laura stared at him. 'Kit's a good rider?'

He snorted. 'She ain't good, she fantastic. The best. Eighteen months ago, she Rising Star of the Year at Kentucky Horse Park's Annual Show. The other youngsters, they go green with envy. She took home all trophies for her age group. Jumped like a superstar. But her heart, always it has been in racing. She dream of being jockey since she knee high to grasshopper. But not any more. Not since accident. Now . . .'

He lifted his hands in a helpless gesture. 'Now, no one can get through to her. The Wainrights, they feel they are responsible. Their hearts are broken. She like daughter to them, you know. I tell them, no one can see inside the mind of a horse. It was accident, end a story.'

'What happened?' asked Laura. In the distance, Kit was kneeling beside the bike. She stood up and began pushing it back to the house.

Roberto leaned against the paddock rails. He lowered his voice. 'She was exercising horse for Mr Wainright and the trainer, Mitch. But this horse was special one. She ride Red Bishop, favourite for Kentucky Derby one year ago. Plenty people, including me, warn Mr Wainright against putting young girl on these fast, powerful horses, but he always say Kit had best instincts of any exercise rider he knew. It is true. Difficult horse, they go like dream for her. They love her and she love them. Not any more, a course, but in them days.'

Tariq moved closer. 'So what went wrong?'

Roberto opened his big, dry hands. 'Only God knows. Kit and Bishop were on last furlong of the gallops, easing up like Mitch tol' them, when all of a sudden that horse went crazy.'

Into Laura's mind came an image of Noble Warrior exploding into fury the previous morning. 'Did something startle him?'

Roberto shook his head. 'No one saw nothing. Maybe

he lose his mind. He threw Kit and bolted for boundary fence' – he nodded towards the horizon – 'way down the end of farm. Beyond is old limestone quarry. Very dangerous. Giant cliffs. Nobody go there but that fool boy, Ivan. The gate between has chain and lock. That day it was open. Red Bishop he slip and break leg. Terrible business. *Terrible.*

'Kit, she was just bruised, not hurt, but for three weeks she not speak one word. When she finally talk she tell her Grandpa it all her fault that Red Bishop die and she never want to ride again. She say she hate every horse. We tell her it's not true till we blue in face, but she not listen to anyone.'

He looked quite bereft. 'She and I, we good friends once. She always under my feet, wanting to play with foals, wanting me teach her training tricks. Now I don't see her no more. She always in the house, always sad.'

Laura stroked the nose of the palomino. Her heart went out to Roberto as much as to the silent girl. Who could blame Kit for not wanting to be around horses? An event like that would traumatise anyone. 'Kit said something about the horses being the cause of all the trouble around here.'

Roberto stared at her broodingly. 'She did? She right, I s'pose. See, Red Bishop, he belong to our neighbour, Nathan Perry. He Mr Wainright's best friend. When Bishop broke leg, he sue Mr and Mrs Wainright for many millions of dollars. He say Blake and Mitch very negligent putting a child on his champion horse. Before that, the Wainrights own farm outright. Now the bank are every day calling to scream for money. Blake and Nathan, they don't speak no more.'

'But what about Gold Rush?' Tariq wanted to know. 'If he's worth $75 million, couldn't they sell him?'

Roberto shook his head. 'Goldie not owned by Wainwright family. He belongs to syndicate of lotsa businessmen. The Wainrights love him like their own precious child, but they have only one tiny piece of him. We had many promising mares and foals here, but all were sold to raise money for lawsuit. The ones you see here are only boarding at Fleet Farm. But it wasn't enough. Lawyers, you know, these people eat money. The Wainrights' only hope is Noble Warrior. He the one racehorse that belongs just to them. If he doesn't win Derby, they lose farm for sure.'

Tariq thought of the money Blake had donated to their St Ives' school. If he was short of cash, he must have parted with the money only because he was expecting a miracle in return. Tariq's stomach gave a nervous heave. No pressure then.

The faint squeak of brakes warned of Kit's approach. Perhaps realising that he'd said more than he should have, Roberto gave a guilty start.

'Thanks, Roberto,' Laura said loudly. 'You've been a huge help.'

He smiled gratefully. 'No problem, Miss Laura. You have fun riding Honey. She a honey. Most gentle horse on farm. Your horse is call Braveheart, Tariq. Brave his name, brave his nature. Enjoy!'

Kit propped her bike against the mounting block. Her hair was sticking up in every direction and she was wearing ripped jeans, a checked shirt and a cowboy hat. She made no attempt to approach the horses. 'Sorry I'm late. Flat tyre.'

Her voice was gruff and it was obvious it took effort for her to apologise to them. 'You ready?'

'Yes, we are,' responded Laura, feeling very much warmer towards the girl than she had done only ten minutes earlier. 'We're looking forward to it.'

12

WHATEVER KIT'S FEELINGS about horses or annoying visitors who got in the way of her reading and guitar playing, she was a superb teacher. In no time at all, Tariq and Laura had been taught how to mount and hold the reins properly, Western-style, and had mastered the basics of the rising trot. Kit managed to give most instructions from her bike, but she did have to dismount to adjust their stirrup length.

The day had dawned cold and misty, but as they rode across the farm the clouds cleared to reveal a peacock blue sky. The sun beat down pleasantly on Laura's fair skin. Her palomino mare, Honey, was a dream to ride. Sweet and willing. Beside her, Tariq couldn't stop grinning. He'd taken to horse riding like a dolphin to the waves. His skewbald pony stepped out keenly, ears pricked.

Kit cycled ahead, leading them past emerald pastures and along a sandy road to the training track – an all-weather surface made of sand, carpet, wax and shredded tyres on which the horses were put through their paces every morning. As they neared it, Ivan emerged from behind a stone wall leading a black colt. He was wearing a Fleet Farm jacket and a billowing pair of yellow and blue polka-dotted pants. A disembodied voice shouted after him. 'Lazy good for nothing! You're wearing out my last nerve Ivan. One more mess up and you're out.'

'Greetings, my friends!' he cried cheerfully. He touched his forelock. 'Hey, Kit, zat is a good horse you are riding. More reliable than zis one and no sweat!'

Kit gave a weak smile, but it was obvious that she didn't appreciate his attempt at humour. 'Hi Ivan. What have you been doing to upset Mitch this time?'

He grinned and shrugged. 'I never do nothing. He get out the bed on the wrong side. Working wiz Mitch is like knowing a tiger wiz a sorn in his paw. Okay, kids, see you. Must keep zis baby moving.'

'Is Ivan an exercise rider?' Laura asked when he'd gone. She couldn't imagine that his billowing pants were very suitable for racing across the farm on the back of a one-ton animal. They'd have a parachute effect.

Kit gave a rude laugh. 'Ivan ride? He couldn't stay on a rocking horse. No, he's what's known as a hotwalker. When the exercise riders are done, the hotwalker cools the horses down by walking 'em and hosing 'em down.

The reason Mitch is always on his case is 'cos Ivan spends any spare moment he gets juggling, turning somersaults or working on his fitness in the old quarry. He takes a stopwatch. He's obsessed with improving his running times.'

At the mention of the quarry, a shadow passed across her face. As if suddenly remembering that she wasn't supposed to be enjoying herself, she said huffily: 'Stop dawdling. I haven't got all day. I'll show you the track and then we're returning to the barn. I'm not a tour guide, you know.'

Beneath Laura, Honey had begun to fuss and fret. Laura wondered if the black colt had upset her. She stroked the mare's satiny gold neck. It worked momentarily, but as they passed through the gate and saw the circular track, Honey became increasingly distressed, especially when Mitch's red truck roared to life. With a wave of his hand, the trainer drove off in the direction of the house and barns. He'd finished work for the morning.

Honey threw up her head, showing the whites of her eyes. 'What do I do, Kit?' called Laura, alarmed.

Kit, who'd ridden her bike to the track's edge, braked with a grimace. But when she saw how Honey was playing up, her expression changed to concern. 'Keep calm, Laura. Try not to let her know you're nervous. Keep your hands down and still. Don't jab her in the mouth. You'll be fine.'

But Laura was not fine. Something was seriously wrong with Honey. Lather was collecting like foam on the mare's flanks. Her ears were back and she was snorting and threatening to rear.

Tariq tried to manouevre his horse alongside her so that he could grab Honey's reins, but Braveheart refused to cooperate.

Kit laid down her bike carefully so as not to frighten the mare further. 'Hold on, Laura,' she said in a calm, authoritative voice, sounding much older than her years. 'Don't worry. I'm not going to allow anything to happen to you, I promise.'

It was easier said than done. Hardly had the words left her mouth than Honey wheeled on the spot, almost sending Laura flying. Then she bolted.

Laura caught a glimpse of Tariq's frightened face as she hurtled by, clinging to Honey's mane. She hauled desperately on the reins, but to no avail. Honey had the bit between her teeth and was galloping along the dirt road beside the track as if the hounds of hell were on her trail. Faster and faster they flew. Laura tried to follow Kit's advice and pretend she wasn't scared, but it was no use. She was terrified.

Ahead lay the quarry. Roberto had said that the gate was always kept locked, but what if it had been left open as it had been on the day of Kit's accident? Would Honey sense danger and stop? Or would she race on until she reached the giant cliffs Roberto had described, carrying them both to their doom? The beloved faces of her uncle, Tariq and Skye came into Laura's head. What if she ended up in hospital with multiple fractures? Worse still, what if something happened and she never saw them again?

The thunder of the mare's hooves roared in Laura's head. It seemed to be getting louder. As they tore towards the boundary fence, Laura tried once more to stop her. Honey responded by speeding up. As they drew nearer, Laura saw that her worst fears were realised. The gate was ajar.

'No!' she cried as Honey swerved through. Already half out of the saddle, she only narrowly avoided being catapulted into a thorn bush by the mare's corkscrew turn. Before them lay the gaping expanse of the quarry, its sheer cliffs dropping away to reveal a white valley in which rainwater had formed deep blue pools. As Honey raced blindly towards the edge of the void, shale spat like sparks from her flying feet.

Laura's life flashed before her eyes. They were going to die and there was not a thing she could do about it. A kind of numb acceptance stole into her veins. Then the faces of Skye, Tariq and her uncle flashed through her mind and she rallied once more. She had to fight until her last breath to save herself – and Honey. Weakly, she gathered the reins.

Over the clatter of hooves came an echo, a staccato rhythm that grew louder and louder. Braveheart's head came into view, alongside Laura's hip. His eyes were wide with fear but he galloped at full stretch towards the abyss. Laura risked a glance sideways. Kit was on his back, driving him on. As Braveheart drew level, the American girl reached out and grabbed Honey's bridle.

'Hold tight, Laura,' she yelled. Pulling with all her strength, she steered the horses away from the crumbling edge, turning them in a tight circle until Honey's wild flight slowed and the sweating palomino came to a shaky-legged halt.

Kit was on the ground and at Laura's side in a second. Laura toppled from the saddle, collapsing into the American girl's arms. As she did so, there was a low rumble and the section of cliff across which they'd just galloped broke off and plunged into the valley. The rocks pelted the limestone basin far below. The girls stared at each other in shock. Before they could react, Tariq, whose horse had been commandeered by Kit, came flying up to them on the bike.

'Laura, Kit, thank God you're okay.' There was a catch in his voice. He flung the bike down. There was a split second of awkwardness and then the three of them were hugging and sobbing with relief.

The man who watched from the trees saw the trio clinging together in an unbroken circle.

13

'I GUESS INSTINCT just took over.'

Hours after her heroic rescue of Laura, Kit was still stunned at what had happened – not because she'd done the impossible and snatched Laura and Honey from the extreme edge of a disintegrating cliff, but rather because she'd found the courage to ride a horse again.

Tariq had described her recruitment of Braveheart with laughing admiration. 'One minute I was watching Honey streak away into the distance at a million miles an hour and feeling totally helpless, and the next Kit was virtually pulling me out of the saddle. She told me not to worry because she was going to save you if it killed her.'

88

'And it almost did,' Laura said with a shudder. 'I'll never be able to thank you enough for saving my life, Kit, but I feel very guilty when I think how close you came to going over the edge yourself.'

Kit giggled. 'Don't feel guilty. It wasn't that close. There were at least six centimetres between us and the abyss!'

The teenager was sitting cross-legged on her bed in her rather untidy room with her newfound friends. And they *were* friends. How could they not be after what they'd been through together? Across her lap lay an acoustic guitar, on which she absent-mindedly strummed a country song as they talked, and all around the room were piles of mystery and adventure books. The transformation in her was quite extraordinary. It was as if someone had reached inside her and switched a light on.

Her grandparents had been quite awestruck by the change. A groundsman had spotted Honey bolt and had radioed the house to alert them. They'd come racing to the quarry expecting to find three children in various states of injury or anguish and instead found them falling about laughing. What had set them off was a comment by Tariq. He'd been describing Kit's impressive mounting technique to Laura.

'She was on Braveheart's back in a single bound, and boy did he understand that the situation was urgent. He couldn't have galloped any faster if his tail was on fire.'

Perhaps because they'd been so close to disaster and had survived, they were euphoric. Everything seemed funny to them. But the reaction of the Wainrights and Garth Longbrook, who'd come tearing up to them in the

Fleet Farm truck and leapt out anticipating the worst was sobering. Christine had flung her arms around each of them in turn. Her eyes were red and she was shaking. 'Thank goodness you're all right,' she kept saying. 'Thank goodness you're all right.'

Blake had apologised to Laura at least a hundred times about the behaviour of Honey, supposedly the safest horse on the farm. 'I can't understand it,' he said over and over. 'I'm mystified. I can only imagine that a bee stung her. I'm so sorry, Laura. What you and Tariq must think of us. We've invited you to Fleet Farm for a relaxing holiday and so far you've had a couple of sleepless nights, narrowly avoided being trampled by Noble Warrior and almost been catapulted over a cliff by Honey. It wasn't how I planned to thank you for rescuing Goldie.'

Garth Longbrook's main concern was that the quarry gate had been left open. He'd glared at Laura as if she were somehow responsible. 'Three times I've bought a lock for it and three times it's been broken and removed,' he said angrily. 'If I catch the person who's doing it, they'll be banned from Fleet Farm for life. As soon as I get back to my office, I'm calling the security company and getting them to put a CCTV camera and an alarm on this section of fence.'

Christine had wanted to radio Roberto and ask him to lead the horses back to the barn, but Kit insisted that she, Laura and Tariq were perfectly capable of doing it themselves. That was how Laura came to find the cause of the palomino's frenzied flight. She was unbuckling Honey's bridle when a small plastic phial dropped out of the hollow of the mare's browband. Kit had turned away to undo the mare's girth so she didn't notice Laura pick it up and, acting on instinct, sniff it. The phial was nearly empty but the few drops of orange liquid that remained smelled the same as the sleeve of the jacket that had so enraged Noble Warrior. It smelled of wildcat. It smelled like a predator.

As she put it in her pocket and covered it with her hand, Laura noticed something interesting. The plastic softened as it warmed. It was then that it hit her that the whole thing had been planned. Someone had put the phial in Honey's browband knowing that as the horse got hotter the plastic would pop, dribble down the palomino's nose and release the wildcat odour guaranteed to drive even the most docile horse out of its mind. The fact that the quarry gate had been left open was too much of a coincidence. Someone had meant to harm Laura. But why?

The only possible conclusion was that she, like Tariq, was a threat. Tariq because he potentially had the special touch that could help Noble Warrior win the Derby, and Laura because . . . well, because she had a reputation as an ace investigator. Those were Blake's words, not hers.

'I've told everyone at Fleet Farm that Britain's best girl detective is coming to stay,' he'd said with a grin on the night before they flew to the US. 'Not that there'll be any mysteries for you to solve now that Goldie has been found – well, apart from the matter of who abducted him, but it never hurts to have an extra pair of eyes around the place. There are still a lot of unanswered questions about why the horse was stolen in the first place.'

Laura had followed Kit into the house with that thought weighing heavily on her mind. Goldie's thieves might be behind bars, but they may not have acted alone. Clearly there was someone, or several people, at Fleet Farm who didn't want anyone – not even a couple of kids – nosing around.

When Kit nipped into the kitchen to fetch three glasses of iced lemonade, Laura took the opportunity to update Tariq on the phial hidden in Honey's bridle. She'd already told him about the wildcat scent she'd found on the jacket.

Now, sitting on Kit's bed, she realised that in order to get at the truth she had to test their fragile new friendship. Picking nervously at a thread on her jeans, she said: 'Kit, would you mind if I asked you about your accident?'

The American girl flinched as if she'd been struck. She drew in an uneven breath. 'What would you like to know?'

'What exactly happened?'

Kit put aside her guitar and hugged her knees. 'It was a year ago today. That's what makes it so weird. It's almost as if some twist of fate meant you to have an accident on the anniversary of mine.'

Laura looked at Tariq but made no comment. 'Go on.'

Kit gave a sweet smile that softened her face. Her hair was still sticking up all over the place, but she'd put on a pink T-shirt and cropped khaki pants. Laura noticed for the first time that she was actually very pretty.

'I was helping Gramps prepare Nathan Perry's stallion, Red Bishop, for the Derby. It was sort of our tradition. I'd wanted to be a jockey since before I could walk and I'd always dreamed of riding at Churchill Downs – that's the home of the Derby. No one encouraged me more than Gramps. Even when I was a little kid, he'd discuss training methods with me and talk about form – how a horse is performing. That's important, but even when they're running poorly no horse is ever just a number to Gramps. Each of them is special in their own way.

'As I grew older and stronger, Gramps would let me exercise some of the racehorses. He used to say that there was no creature on earth that responded to honesty and kindness like a thoroughbred.

'On that particular day, Mitch, the trainer, was having a lot of trouble with Red Bishop. Bishop's usual exercise rider had been fired and he hadn't taken to the new man at all. I'd ridden him a few times and he'd always been an angel with me so Gramps decided on the spur of the moment that I should take him out that morning. Mitch was really adamant I shouldn't, particularly with the Derby so close. They almost came to blows over it. Mitch said it was the worst idea he'd ever heard. He wanted to check with Nathan – he's our neighbour and he used to be Gramps' best friend – but Gramps can be pretty stubborn and he said that what Nathan knew about training wouldn't fit on a postage stamp.

'Mitch stormed off but he came back about five minutes later in a really good mood. Gramps told him that he wanted me to ride Bishop and if Mitch didn't like it he could put it in his pipe and smoke it. The strange thing was that Mitch told him he thought it was a great idea if I took Bishop out and there was no need for Gramps to get so stroppy about it.'

'When did you first realise that something was wrong?' asked Tariq.

'Around the second furlong. Bishop was a big horse but he'd always been a gentle giant. It's a cliché, but in his case it was true. I'd always loved to watch him run. It was as if he went into this happy place in his head.'

She smiled at the memory, but her face quickly clouded. 'He galloped like a dream for the first part of his workout, but then he began to fidget. I could tell that something was upsetting him, I just couldn't figure out what. Come to think of it, he was behaving a bit like Honey did before she bolted. I kept thinking that he'd relax once he got into his stride. Instead he began to gallop as though he was being pursued by a hungry mountain lion. I tried to pull him up on the last furlong and he seemed to be slowing. Then all of sudden he went berserk.'

Tears filled her eyes. 'That's all I remember. When I came round, Gramps told me that Red Bishop had broken a leg in the quarry and they'd had to put him to sleep.'

She said passionately: 'I'll never forgive myself. I made up my mind that I'd never ride again, never so much as touch a horse. And I haven't. Until today.'

Laura said: 'Maybe it wasn't your fault – what happened with Bishop, I mean.'

'You sound like Grandma and Gramps. That's what they're always telling me.'

'Well, perhaps they're right.'

Kit shook her head violently. 'No. No, they're not. I

shouldn't have been riding him. I'm responsible for kill
. . . for killing—'

'Was there anything unusual about Red Bishop when
he was found?' Tariq interrupted. 'I know he was badly
injured, but did the vet or anyone else mention anything
peculiar? Did they notice a funny smell on his bridle or
saddlecloth, for instance?'

Kit went rigid. She stared at Tariq as if he'd suddenly
grown two heads. 'How could you know that?' she
demanded. 'Who have you been talking to?'

'Just tell us,' Laura said gently. 'It's important.'

Kit was pale. 'All I know is that the veterinarian told Ken
that Red Bishop's bridle had a really strange odour when
they removed it. He said it smelled like a bear's lair or a
cougar, like some wild creature. He questioned how the
smell had got there, but I don't think anyone paid much
attention at the time. They were too preoccupied by the
loss of the Derby favourite.'

The blood roared in Laura's ears. She'd been expecting
to hear something of the kind, but having it confirmed
made her feel ill. 'Kit, what would you say if I told you that
you're not responsible for Red Bishop's death? That I'm
pretty sure that what happened to you wasn't an accident.'

Kit snorted. 'I'd assume you were making a really
bad joke. What are you trying to tell me? That someone
wanted to hurt me or destroy Bishop? That his bridle was
sabotaged in some way?'

'That's exactly what I'm saying,' Laura told her. 'And I
can prove it.'

14

'WHERE DO WE BEGIN?' Kit wanted to know.

The three were sitting on a rise behind the mares' and foals' barn, shaded by an old oak hung with Spanish moss. Laura could not decide whether the effect was gorgeous or ghostly. Scattered on the rug before them were the remains of a picnic lunch of po-boys – delicious crusty rolls stuffed with fried green tomatoes, cheese and spicy mayonnaise. They were accompanied by root beer, a drink that tasted like bubblegum and wasn't beer at all. For dessert, there were homemade red velvet cupcakes with vanilla icing.

Before coming outside Laura had shown Kit the little plastic container she'd found in Honey's bridle.

Unfortunately, the remaining drops of orange liquid had leaked out and it no longer smelled of wildcat. Even more unfortunately, the jacket Tariq had been wearing when Noble Warrior attacked him had been washed. Once again Kit and Tariq had to take Laura's word for what she'd seen and smelled.

Nevertheless, Kit had helped Laura hide the phial, carefully wrapped in an 'evidence' bag, in the back of the Wainrights' vast refrigerator in order to preserve it for possible testing.

Much to Laura's relief, Kit hadn't dismissed the sabotage theory out of hand. In fact, she'd taken it very seriously.

'It sounds far-fetched. I mean, what kind of monster would do such a thing?' was her initial reaction. But she admitted that three accidents taking place on one farm, all apparently caused by a wild animal smell, was too much of a coincidence. Especially when one took into account the theft of Goldie.

Laura couldn't help thinking that this was the second time she'd been promised a dream holiday which had rapidly turned into a nightmare. Her Caribbean adventure had begun the same way. One minute she and Tariq were looking forward to a blissful couple of weeks on a snowy white island surrounded by turquoise waters and the next they were at risk of being devoured by sharks or incinerated by a flaming volcano. This vacation was showing every sign of going the same way. Each time Laura relived the moment when Honey accelerated towards the cliff edge, she shivered. Beneath its pristine, lovely surface, there were dark forces at work at Fleet Farm.

'According to Gramps, you've both had plenty of experience with investigations,' Kit was saying between bites of cupcake. 'You know about this stuff. With the Derby coming up in four days, my grandparents have way too many worries already. If you don't mind, I'd rather that we kept this a secret between us for the moment. With any luck, there's a simple explanation and we can clear it up on our own. Is that a deal?'

'You have our word,' Tariq said.

'Deal,' agreed Laura, feeling a pang of guilt when she recalled again her promise to her uncle. But as Kit said, there was probably a simple explanation for the odd goings on at Fleet Farm. There was no sense in causing unnecessary stress to the Wainwrights or her uncle when they could clear the mystery up on their own.

Kit wiped her mouth with a napkin. For a girl who'd just been told that somebody had tried to do grievous bodily harm to either her or Red Bishop, she looked strangely excited. 'Right, where do we begin?'

Tariq put down his root beer and took a notebook from his pocket. He was wearing a black Fleet Farm polo shirt and olive-green cargo shorts. His feet were bare. 'We need a who, why and how list. Who are our main suspects for each incident? What motive could they have? How did they plan it so that each event looked like an accident?'

'Exactly,' agreed Laura. 'Kit, who stood to gain last year if you or Red Bishop were harmed?'

Kit lay back on the grass with her hands behind her head. 'Me? Nobody. Red Bishop is a different story. He was hot favourite for the Derby. Any time a dead cert doesn't win a major race, lots of people benefit. A gambler or a bookmaker who stood to lose a lot of money on him might have wanted him stopped. So might a trainer who wanted a different horse to win.'

'What about your neighbour, Nathan Perry?' Laura asked.

Kit sat up. 'Don't be nutty. Nathan was Bishop's owner. There wouldn't have been a prouder man in the whole of Kentucky if his stallion had won the Derby. Especially because of what happened with Noble Warrior and Valiant.'

Tariq put down his pen. 'What do you mean?'

'Haven't you heard? You see, Gramps and Nathan were joint owners of Noble's dam. That's what we call a horse's mother – the dam. When they discovered she was expecting twins, they agreed to toss a coin to decide who took which foal. Nathan got Valiant, a good horse but not a great one. He could barely outrun Honey. Gramps got Noble Warrior, who's grown up to be one of the best racehorses in America. He's odds-on favourite for the Derby.'

The word 'revenge' came into Laura's head, but she didn't say it out loud. 'Let's put a question mark after Nathan's name. He could well have been nursing a grudge for years.'

Kit's eyes widened as a thought occurred to her. 'What if someone is trying to destroy my grandfather? Someone besides Nathan, I mean. Before the lawsuit, Fleet Farm was one of the most successful racing operations in the country. Whoever hurt Bishop must have known that

Gramps' reputation would be damaged and he'd end up with loads of debts.'

Laura was impressed. 'That's the kind of deduction Matt Walker would make. He's a fictional detective, but he's always coming up with super-smart theories. But don't be too quick to dismiss Nathan. It's hard to imagine that anyone could be wicked enough to injure their own horse, but remember that Red Bishop wasn't guaranteed to win the Derby. He could have finished last. On the other hand, by suing your grandfather Nathan could end up owning Fleet Farm.'

Kit bit her lip and said nothing.

Tariq wrote Nathan's name on his pad below 'gamblers' and 'bookmakers.' He also wrote, 'Somebody may be out to get Fleet Farm at all costs,' and tucked the pen behind his ear. 'Okay, let's turn to the events of the last couple of days – Noble Warrior attacking us and Honey going berserk? We're strangers here and we're just kids. Why would anyone want us out of the way?'

'Because there's something they don't want found,' Kit answered. 'But who or what it might be, I haven't a clue. I like everyone who works on Fleet Farm.'

Tariq's pen was poised over his notebook. His skin looked like burnt honey in the dappled sunlight and his amber eyes were serious. *'Everyone?'*

'Well, nearly everyone. Mitch is all right, but it annoys me that he's always being mean to Ivan, who's fun and cool. He's also always complaining about being short of money. Ryan once told me he has a brother who's forever in trouble or out of work and borrowing cash from him.

But Gramps won't hear a word against Mitch. Says there's no better trainer.

'Ken has been like a bear with a sore head ever since Ryan was beaten up by Goldie's abductors, but he loves horses more than anything in the world. I can't imagine him laying a finger on one. You saw how upset he was about what happened with you and Honey today.'

And they had. He'd come rushing out to greet them as they'd led the horses back to the stables, looking as if he was about to burst into tears. 'I'm so sorry you've had to go through this, Laura,' he said. 'I'm so sorry, Tariq. Kit, if something had happened to you I . . . I . . . If something . . . This is bad. This is so bad.'

He'd offered to untack their horses and rub them down. When Kit had told him that they'd prefer do it themselves, he'd stumbled away looking more downcast than ever.

Lost in thought, Laura took a swig of her root beer.

'Garth Longbrook is hardly likely to be involved,' Kit was telling Tariq. 'He's our head of security.'

Laura had her own opinion of Garth Longbrook, but she decided to keep it to herself. She gazed out at the yearlings that dotted the green pasture nearest them. Any one of them could grow into a legend like Eclipse, or Seabiscuit, or Secretariat. Across the globe, owners, trainers and jockeys competed to spot that special horse using science, psychics or any other means available in a race as intense as any on track. Over the centuries, it had driven many men mad.

She shielded her eyes from the sun. On the horizon, a lone figure was running in the direction of the quarry. It was Ivan, on his way to do his sprint training, despite the heat of the day. Odd that a young man with a reputation for idleness should be so obsessed with physical fitness.

'What about Roberto?' Tariq suggested. 'He saddled Honey. It's unlikely to be him because it's so obvious, but I have to ask.'

Kit laughed. 'Never. Not in a million years. Roberto has worked for Gramps for about twenty years. He's the gentlest soul I've ever met.'

She looked at Laura. 'I'm not sure that you'll ever solve this mystery. Dozens of people come and go every single day at Fleet Farm. Owners, exercise riders, grooms and trainers. It could be any one of them.'

Laura smiled. There was a point in every Matt Walker novel where the list of potential suspects seemed infinite and the riddle insoluble. 'It could be any of them, but it isn't. The truth is staring us in the face. We only have to know how to look for it. Try not to worry. If we're patient, we'll get to the bottom of this. What I'd really like to know is how the culprit got hold of the wildcat scent.'

'If that's what it is,' pointed out Kit, who had yet to be convinced about the cause of the accidents or the origin of the odour.

'A zoo,' suggested Tariq, writing it down.

'How about a pet tiger?' Kit volunteered. 'Thousands of Americans keep tigers in their apartments or backyards. There are bound to be a few in Kentucky.'

Laura was aghast. 'But that's cruel. Wild tigers are almost extinct. They are meant to be free and living in jungles, far from humans. They are meant to hunt and roam and raise their cubs. They don't belong in living rooms.'

'I agree, but lots of people think differently. Okay, what else?'

'I don't suppose there are any circuses in town?' asked Tariq.

Kit knocked her root beer over. It gushed onto the rug and soaked the last bite of her cupcake but she didn't appear to notice. 'There was a European circus in Lexington for Derby week last year, right around the time of my accident. The same circus is on again this week. The billboard advertising it has a photo of a tiger leaping through a hoop of fire. They call themselves Rock The Big Top.'

Laura's pulse quickened. She'd learned the hard way that coincidences often turned out to be nothing of the kind. Ordinarily, she loathed circuses that used animals and would have walked across flaming coals to avoid them, but she'd be failing Kit if she didn't pursue such a strong lead. 'How difficult would it be for us to get to this circus? Somehow we have to find a way to go.'

Kit went red. 'We're already going. Grandma told me that she'd bought tickets as a surprise for us when I was setting out to the stables this morning, only I didn't say anything because I was still furious with you and Tariq for coming here and ruining my vacation. I was planning to wriggle out of it if I possibly could.'

Laura glanced sideways. 'And you don't feel like that now.'

'Of course not,' said Kit, dabbing inadequately at the rug with a paper napkin. 'Now I think that you're pretty amazing and that I've been the world's biggest moron. I only hope you can forgive me. We're going to the circus tomorrow night. If there are any villains there, I plan to help you track them down.'

15

THE ROCK THE BIG TOP circus had a candy-striped tent and an old-fashioned merry-go-round with quaint plumed horses, but in every other way it was a cutting-edge show. In the first half alone they saw sky-walking acrobats, trapeze artists flying without wings, or indeed harnesses, and a magician who made a peacock disappear. Some eye-popping feats seemed more suited to science fiction than real life.

They were dazzled by a swarthy man in a billowing white shirt, who encased himself in swirling twists of flaming rope; by a juggler who tossed fizzing fireworks; and by a beautiful dancer who flowed like mercury over, under and through the legs of two shimmering white unicorns. For her final trick, she did a backflip off one and landed lightly on the rump of the other.

'They're not real unicorns, of course, they're Andalucian stallions from Spain by the look of them,' Blake Wainwright told Laura as they filed out into the darkness for the interval. 'But they look like the real thing and how superbly they performed. What exquisite creatures.'

He looked at his watch. 'Now if you'll excuse me, I need to find somewhere quiet so I can phone the farm. With only days to go until the Derby, we're on tenterhooks in case some fool takes it into his head to steal Noble Warrior or get at him in some way. Garth's pulling out every stop to make the stallion barn as secure as a bank vault.'

Christine waved him off vaguely and beamed at the children. She was so overjoyed that her withdrawn, taciturn granddaughter was once again laughing and communicative that she wouldn't have minded if the show had featured eight decrepit mules. That it had been quite breathtaking was a bonus. 'I don't know about you, but I need to powder my nose. Would anyone else—?'

'We're fine,' Kit said quickly. She, Laura and Tariq were determined to do as much snooping around as possible during the short interval. 'Why don't you give us our tickets and we'll meet you back in the tent? We thought we might check out the Haunted House.'

Christine's smiled faded. They'd passed the gothic mansion while exploring the amusement park earlier and it had looked quite horrible – like some sort of ghostly, ghastly stage set. 'Are you sure that's a good idea, sweetie?'

'Only briefly,' Kit assured her, 'and then we'll be going for candy floss.'

Christine glanced at the queue forming outside the ladies' bathroom and decided that the sooner she joined it the better. She rummaged in her purse for some dollars and handed them to Kit. 'All right, dear, but please don't do anything that gives our guests nightmares. Remember that Laura's already had to cope with a runaway horse. I'm sure she and Tariq have had quite enough drama for one trip.'

As soon as she'd turned her back, they slipped into the lively crowd. Fairground rides twisted and spun overhead, creating a kaleidoscope of colour against the night sky. White and blue strobe lights raked the darkness. The noise was deafening. Pop music competed with shrieking rollercoaster passengers and the music box blare of the merry-go-round. Laura was entranced, if a little dizzy. The swirling lights and general cacophony made the ground beneath her feet feel curiously unstable. She inhaled a lungful of burger smoke and the burnt sugar scent of candyfloss and caramelised nuts.

Towards the rear of the grounds it was quieter, apart from the screams emanating from the Haunted House. As they neared it, a couple of white-faced boys burst from a side door, followed by two girls bent double with laughter. Much teasing of the boys ensued. Laura didn't blame them for being scared. The exterior of the fake mansion was spooky enough. Spiders lurked in the cobwebs dangling from the porch and the yellow attic windows seemed to stare down at her like watching eyes.

She dreaded to think what the interior was like.

Contrary to what Kit had told her grandmother, the children had no intention of visiting the Haunted House. They were more interested in the caravans and animal trailers that lay behind it, partially concealed by a wall of white sheeting. There was no obvious security. After a short search, Tariq found a flap hanging loose. Judging by the number of cigarette butts on the ground, they were not the first to use it as an access route.

Kit went first, followed by Tariq. Laura brought up the rear. She was pulling the flap closed behind her when she caught a glimpse of Ivan. Fleet Farm's hotwalker had as much right to visit the circus as anyone else, but for some reason Laura's internal radar began to beep. Ivan rounded the front of the Haunted House and vanished from view.

She said hurriedly: 'I think we should split up. We've only got twenty minutes and we'll cover more ground. I'll meet you back in the main tent.'

Before Kit or Tariq could object, she'd ducked under the flap and was gone.

Kit shook her head in wonder. 'Is she always like this?'

'Like what?' asked Tariq.

'Like a beagle on the scent when she has a mystery to solve?'

Tariq grinned. 'She has a nose for trouble if that's what you mean. Her uncle was once one of the best detectives in Britain and Laura takes after him. Now, we don't have much time. Let's try to find the tiger trailer.'

In the thirty seconds it took Laura to reach the Haunted House, Ivan had disappeared. She scanned the nearby crowds but there was no sign of him. The front door of the gothic mansion was squeaking on its hinges. Could he have gone in there? The thought of entering the spider-plagued house made every hair on Laura's body stand on end, but she didn't see any alternative. Ivan had been striding along like a man on a mission. He didn't have the look of someone who was merely enjoying a night out at the circus.

She wished now that she hadn't been so hasty in sending Kit and Tariq away, but she also knew that she had more chance of remaining undetected if she tracked Ivan on her own. She glanced around in the hope of seeing other children and/or parents on their way to the Haunted House. It would be easier to cope with if there were. Unfortunately, families tended to veer away as they approached it. Perhaps the screams of previous victims had put them off.

She hurried to the ticket booth and handed over five dollars. The old crone at the counter, made up to look like a witch, did not inspire confidence. She fixed a glass eye on Laura and croaked: 'Without yer Mum 'n' Dad? Yer a brave one.' When Laura nodded, she cackled.

It's just part of the act, Laura decided. Nothing to do with me. Nothing to worry about.

She took her ticket and crossed the gravel path to the

house. Turning a blind eye to a pair of very realistic looking tarantulas, she walked determinedly up the porch steps and pushed open the front door. All she had to do was tell herself that nothing she saw or heard was real. Everything was for show. The ghosts would be projected lights or out-of-work actors wrapped in sheets.

Once inside, it became much harder to keep a grip on reality. It was pitch black for starters. She literally couldn't see her hand in front of her face. She'd hoped that a couple of previous visitors would be lingering there, providing a modicum of comfort, but she was alone with only the piped whine of a mournful wind for company. Mad laughter suddenly boomed in her ear and she almost jumped out of her skin.

Picking cobwebs out of her hair, Laura moved on jelly legs towards the outline of a door. As she passed through it, cold fingers brushed the back of her neck. She thought she heard a whisper: 'Laura, Laura, Laura . . .'

Her heartbeat accelerated and a small scream escaped her, but she managed to force herself on. She found herself in an old living room, spookily lit. A rocking chair began to swing crazily, as if occupied by some unseen person. The wind howled in the chimney. Above the sofa were a series of portraits in gilded frames. Their malevolent gazes followed her across the room. A floorboard creaked behind her. She swung to see a ghostly figure dart across the room before vaporising. Laura consoled herself with her out-of-work actor theory. It was all theatre.

She strained her ears to hear if Ivan was in an upstairs

room, but a very realistic thunderstorm had started up and it was impossible. How she wished she'd brought Tariq with her. Tariq was much stronger than most boys his age, and although he claimed to be ignorant of martial arts and was often painfully shy and quite gentle, she was convinced that he had some Far Eastern self-defence skill up his sleeve and would use it if ever called upon to do so. At any rate, she always felt safe around him.

As she made her way up the stairs, lightning shuddered and thunder crashed. At the top was a hall of mirrors, lit by a flickering gas lamp. The wavering light added to the disorienting effect. The room was full of Lauras, reflected from every angle. Every movement caused her multiple selves to fracture.

There was a scraping noise. A dark figure passed briefly across one of the mirrors, causing a ripple effect, like a stone dropped into a still pond.

'Ivan?' Laura called hopefully, turning in a circle, but no one answered. There was a rustle and a woman's face loomed at her left shoulder. The light flickered out. When it flicked on again, she was alone.

For the first time, real terror seized Laura, because the woman's face was one she knew. The face of someone she'd thought was dead; the face of a monster. 'Where are you?' she shouted. 'Show yourself.' There was mocking laughter and fragments of her tormenter danced from mirror to mirror, too quick for Laura to focus on. Here an eye, here a corner of a black silk skirt, the pocket of a dark red blouse, the tip of a shoe.

'We warned you, Laura Marlin . . .' The voice was barely

audible yet it had the effect on Laura of nails scraping a blackboard.

Just when Laura thought she might faint from fright, the room was flooded with light. A man on a crackling speaker system boomed: 'Ladies and gentlemen, please return to the Big Top and take your seats. This evening's performance will resume in three minutes.'

Laura could have wept with relief. She glanced around the room. She was entirely alone. There was no woman. It must have been her imagination, like everything else. She was about to make a thorough search of the mirrored room when the lights snapped off and she was marooned once more in the dark. It was the final straw. Her nerves could not take another second in the house.

She rushed out onto the landing and clattered down the steps, and that's when she heard Ivan's voice. It was coming from outside. Fear momentarily forgotten, she tried the nearest window. It was sealed shut. At the foot of the stairs was a wooden chest. By standing on it, she was able to peer out through a vent.

She was gazing directly into the performers' car park. More particularly, she was staring straight into the open door of a caravan. It was warmly lit with a golden light and three men were visible. One was dressed in black and had his back to Laura, but she had no difficulty recognizing the others. Arms slung across one another's shoulders, they were laughing in a way that would have persuaded any onlooker that they were not only the best of friends, but held each other in the highest esteem.

They raised their glasses.

'Zis time next week, everysing will be different,' Ivan said, his face alight. 'We will be bright shining stars.'

Mitch laughed. 'I'm not sure if the newspapers will see it that way, but who cares about them. I'm counting on you, mate. Don't you forget it.'

'Shame about za dry run wiz Noble Warrior. Zat was a waste of time.'

'Never you mind about that. I have a plan. A genius one. Will tell you about it later. Foolproof it is.'

Laura suddenly became aware that the speaker system in the Haunted House had been turned off. If anything, the silence was spookier than the thunderstorm or ghostly moans. Footsteps clattered up the porch and a muffled voice called: 'Anyone in here?' Before Laura could move a muscle or cry out, a door slammed shut and keys turned in the lock. She leapt off the trunk and rushed through the darkness, cobwebs coating her face with sticky threads. 'I'm in here,' she yelled. 'Don't leave me. Please don't leave me. Help!'

There was no response. She wrenched at the door and jiggled the handle, but it was immovable. There was a whisper of cloth brushing wood, followed by the flare of a match. Laura felt someone touch her hand and she swung in terror. Before her was the ghoulish face of her nightmares, flickering in the candlelight.

We warned you, Laura Marlin . . .

The edges of Laura's vision wavered then everything went black.

16

'IMAGINE THE ATTENDANT being so irresponsible as to lock the Haunted House while you were still inside it, Laura!' Christine said incredulously as they drove home. 'She must be senile. If Ivan hadn't heard you scream and hadn't run into Tariq, who was searching for you, you might have been stuck in there for the night with the spiders and bats and heaven knows what. It beggars belief. The Rock The Big Top people are lucky we're not planning to sue them.'

'Please,' her husband said wearily, massaging his temples as they stopped at a traffic light. 'I appreciate the distress that this unfortunate incident has caused, but surely we've had enough of lawyers to last a lifetime. I'm only sorry that Laura didn't get to see the second half of the show. It was quite spectacular.'

Sandwiched in the back of the car between her best friend and Kit, who kept giving her protective hugs, Laura was only half listening. Her head still ached. She kept going over and over the sequence of events in her mind, trying to understand what had been real in the Haunted House and what hadn't.

It had been a shock to see Ivan's cheeky face peering down at her when she came round from a dead faint. She'd been expecting to see the woman she dreaded. When she saw Fleet Farm's hotwalker instead, she was confused. She'd suspected him of being up to no good and yet here he was rescuing her. It was a relief when Tariq came rushing up and hugged her so hard that she squeaked.

'What are you doing in locked house?' demanded Ivan. 'Who do zis to you?'

'Don't know, I didn't see them,' mumbled Laura, still slightly dazed. 'Please don't mention it to the Wainwrights.'

Ivan frowned. 'We must call cops and find who do zis wicked sing.'

'Why are *you* here?' Laura interrupted before she could stop herself. 'I mean, what are you doing at the circus?'

He was surprised. 'I come to see za show, like you, but also to see my cousin, Mikhail, from Crimea. He is magician and juggler.' He flashed a grin. 'He teach me many tricks. One day I want my own circus, better than zis one. No more walking sweaty horses.'

'Did you come alone?'

Ivan laughed and put a hand on her shoulder. 'You ask

too many questions, Laura, girl. We must go before za Wainwrights get too worried. But, yes, I come by myself. Who else will come wiz me to circus? Mitch? Give me break. Unless he's come here to check up on me. Zat would be more likely.'

Back at Fleet Farm, Laura and Tariq met in Kit's bedroom for an agreed progress report by torchlight. They were each armed with a mug of hot chocolate topped with marshmallows.

Kit and Tariq had little to tell. They'd got as far as the cage of a poor, depressed tiger before being nabbed by a security guard and escorted like criminals back to the embarrassed Wainrights. When Tariq discovered that Laura had not been seen, he'd waited only until the guard departed before racing out of the tent to find her before anyone could stop him.

For now, however, Tariq was more interested in what Laura had learned in the Haunted House.

'But why would Ivan lie about meeting Mitch?' asked Kit. 'Are you *sure* it was Mitch? You know how much they loathe each other.'

'Yes, I do and yes, I'm certain. But maybe it's an act. Maybe they're friends and they only pretend to hate each other.'

Kit was puzzled. 'For what reason?'

'Right now, I don't have a clue.'

She looked up at their expectant faces. 'There's something I need to tell you both. When I was in the hall of mirrors I saw . . . I *thought* I saw . . . someone I knew. A woman. I hoped it was my imagination playing tricks on me . . .'

'But it wasn't?' guessed Kit.

'No. I knew that when I heard her voice and felt her touch my arm. If I live to be a thousand, I'd never forget the coldness of her hands, like some lizard, or the grating way she speaks, as if she has a clothes peg over her nose.'

There was a catch in her voice. 'But Tariq, I thought she was . . . I thought she was dead.'

Tariq froze. 'J-Janet Rain?'

Kit glanced from one to the other in growing alarm. 'Who is this Janet Rain? You make her sound like a monster.'

'It's worse than that,' Tariq told her, 'because she's just one of many. Janet Rain is the woman who helped kidnap Laura and I in the Caribbean, and would have tortured Laura's uncle to death if she'd had her way. She's a member of a gang of evil masterminds known as the Straight A's. They're responsible for some of the worst crimes on earth. Calvin Redfern calls them a Brotherhood of Monsters. The last time we saw Janet we were escaping from a volcano and I guess we thought – *hoped* – that she was gone forever. The newspapers reported her missing, presumed dead.'

'Well, she's not,' said Laura, pulling herself together. 'She's very much alive and at large. The question is, are the Straight A's in town because they're after us, or are they here to cause havoc during the Kentucky Derby?'

'Or both?' added Tariq, which was of no comfort whatsoever.

~ 17 ~

'I AM QUITE determined that nothing will go wrong today and you will finally start to have the vacation you deserve,' declared Christine at breakfast next morning, a Friday. 'I'm afraid that, at this rate, you'll leave the South with the wrong impression of us entirely. We pride ourselves on our culture, our hospitality and our gentility and you don't appear to have experienced any of those things.'

'That's not true at all,' Laura said warmly. 'You and Mr Wainwright and Kit have been lovely. And Anita's food is utterly delicious.'

Tariq, his mouth full of waffle, nodded enthusiastic

agreement. They'd started with eggs and hash browns and moved on to Anita's speciality.

Christine looked pleased and relieved. 'Well, that's good to hear.' She smiled at her granddaughter. 'I gather you took Tariq and Laura to see Noble Warrior's final workout this morning?'

Kit was positively glowing, but she played down the reason for her happiness like a typical teenager, not wanting to seem uncool. 'It was good. He went pretty well. Yeah, it was all right. And then afterwards we stopped by to give a few carrots to Goldie.'

'That's nice, sweetie. And how was he?'

'Yeah, he was all right.'

Laura turned away to hide a smile. At the track that day, she'd seen a very different side to the American girl. It was the first time Kit had been to watch the horses train since her accident the previous year and she'd been unable to contain her excitement. Laura and Tariq had been treated to a running commentary.

'You guys know about exercise riders, right? They're the unsung heroes of the racing world. The jockeys get all the glory. That's okay because they pilot the greatest horses in the biggest races, they're responsible for the split second decisions that can make or break a career, and they're fire-tested in battle. You get jockeys who've broken every bone in their body, but their guts are forged in steel and they keep going back for more. They're fearless because they have to be, but also because they're addicted to the thrill of it. They need speed!'

She'd nodded towards Ken, emerging from the dawn

mist on Noble Warrior. His reins were loose and he swayed with the stallion in one supple motion.

'We have a couple of full-time exercise riders – Ken and Eddie. The rest are freelance. They get paid per horse. They'll ride six or seven horses a day for maybe five hours. A good exercise rider can make or break a horse, but on Derby Day, when the jockey's being praised to the skies, they hardly ever get a mention. That's okay too. Most exercise riders would do it for free. They gallop for the love of it.'

For Laura and Tariq, crouched by the side of the track, what followed was a revelation. For several magical hours, they watched these passionate horsemen put through their paces awkward two-year-old 'babies', some eager, some naughty, as well as strapping stallions and bucking mares – 'broncing' was Kit's word for it, all with the same calm professionalism.

'If I'm not smart enough to become a vet, I want to be an exercise rider,' Tariq whispered to Laura.

Every horse that flew by was gleaming, sinewy and fast, but even Laura's inexperienced eyes could tell that there was something special about Noble Warrior. The red stallion was one of the smallest horses on the track, and yet he lived up to his reputation for being a pocket rocket. Ken jogged him half a mile up the track before turning back. For a further half mile he held the horse in a slow gallop. Then it was as if he'd flipped a switch. Warrior streaked down the track like a flame across oil.

'The average racehorse can cover around six metres in a single stride,' Kit told them in a hushed tone. 'The legendary stallion, Man o' War covered eight and a half. We think Noble Warrior could get close to that. When all four of his feet are off the ground, he flies like Pegasus.'

It was so awe-inspiring to see Noble Warrior thunder past them, his muscles straining beneath his fiery coat, that Laura felt quite emotional. 'I can see why you love racing so much,' she told Kit. 'It's an adrenalin rush, but it's also something more. The horses have so much power and grace and such big hearts, it sort of touches your soul.'

'I guess it's what people mean by poetry in motion,' said Tariq, equally moved.

Kit nodded fiercely, unable to speak. At last she said huskily: 'And I do. Love it, I mean. All that rubbish I talked about hating the horses and not caring if Goldie was gone for good, it was only because I was hurting so much. I blamed myself for what happened to Red Bishop and the thought that I could never again touch a horse or follow my dream of riding in the Derby, was agony. It made me lash out at everything and everyone, including you and Tariq. I'm so sorry.'

Laura gave her an affectionate punch. 'If you apologise one more time, you really are going to be sorry.'

Ken, standing in his short stirrups, had pulled Warrior up. The horse's nostrils flared red. Dragon-like, he breathed smoke into the chilly morning air. Ken patted him, swung off his back and handed the reins to Ivan, who led the stallion away to cool him down.

'How did he feel?' Kit called as Ken passed them, on his way to collect his next mount. 'Is he ready to take on the best horses in the country?'

Ken's serious face lit up briefly. 'Ready as he'll ever be.'

'What happens if he doesn't win the Kentucky Derby this time around?' Tariq wanted to know. 'Can he try again next year?'

Kit laughed. 'Only three-year-olds can enter the Kentucky Derby, so this is his one chance to claim his place in history. If he doesn't do it now, there won't be a next year because he'll have to be sold, along with every other horse we own. Goldie will have to go too. The bank is hounding Gramps for their money. When Warrior races on Sunday, he won't just be running for the roses or for the glory. He'll be running to save Fleet Farm.'

After breakfast, Tariq went to the stallion barn to help prepare Noble Warrior for his journey later that day to Churchill Downs, the famous home of the Kentucky Derby. Laura excused herself to call her uncle. He was thrilled to hear from her.

'How's it going?'

He sounded so near that Laura felt as if she could reach out and touch him. She wished she could. She'd had an unforgettable morning at the track, but the memory of Janet Rain's cold, clutching hands and her whispered threat, 'We warned you, Laura Marlin,' had haunted her sleep. She'd have done anything for one of her uncle's bone-crushing bear hugs and a lick or two from her beloved husky.

'Great,' responded Laura, 'except that I miss you and Skye terribly.'

His laugh boomed down the line. 'Not as much as we miss you.'

Before he could ask any probing questions, Laura launched into an edited account of the wonders of the circus and described her morning at the track.

'What an amazing experience,' he said. 'I'm sorely tempted to hop on the next plane and fly out for the Derby, but I doubt my boss would agree to it.'

'Oh, why don't you try?' pleaded Laura, her spirits suddenly lifted by the prospect of her uncle flying out to deal with the Straight A's and solve the mysteries at Fleet Farm that had so far eluded her.

'Any other news?' Calvin asked, deftly avoiding the question. 'Staying out of trouble?'

'Doing my best,' Laura said, which was perfectly true. It wasn't her fault if trouble kept finding her. 'Only . . .'

'Yes?'

'Uncle Calvin, do you know what the Straight A gang are up to these days? Have you heard any news?'

'There was a long silence. When he spoke, Calvin Redfern's voice was no longer teasing and warm, but stony and focused, the way it went when he was in work mode. 'Laura, what do you know?'

'Nothing. I thought I saw Janet Rain at the circus, that's all.'

'Let me get this right. You thought you saw one of the world's most wanted women at the circus. Was she a lion tamer? A trapeze artist? Seriously, did you definitely see her or is there some doubt about it?'

'I think I saw her, but I'm not sure.'

There was another silence. 'Do you have any reason to think the Straight A gang are targeting Fleet Farm?'

'No.'

'Well, then put them out of your mind. I'll make some enquiries, but you are to stay as far as possible from anything that might even remotely interest the Straight A gang. I've a good mind to ban you from going to the Kentucky Derby.'

Laura gasped. 'You can't.'

He sighed. 'I wouldn't be so cruel. But Laura, promise me that you and Tariq will stick close to Kit and the Wainrights at all times. Promise me that you'll take great care.'

Laura's shoulders sagged with relief. She smiled into the phone. 'Now that I can definitely do.'

As soon as she'd hung up the phone, Laura walked down to the stables. Kit and Tariq were absorbed with preparing Noble Warrior for his journey to Churchill Downs. They looked up distractedly when she put her head over the stable door before resuming their grooming and feet checking. Laura didn't mind in the least. She wanted to cuddle Goldie, who always seemed pleased to see her, and do a little investigating. Her uncle had warned her to stay away from the Straight A's. There was no law against her helping her friends.

As she'd hoped, the stable office was empty. Lying on the table was the daily logbook. With a quick glance over her shoulder, she opened it. On every page were detailed daily notes on feeding and training written in several hands. On impulse, she turned to the page that dealt with the day after their arrival, in the early hours of which she'd seen the mysterious second lorry and chestnut horse.

Apart from a careful account of Noble Warrior's performance in training that morning and a note that he'd run poorly – in the margin was the comment, 'Hardly surprising, given the disturbance in the night' – but otherwise it contained nothing untoward.

Remembering the conversation she'd overheard at the circus, Laura flicked through the diary to see if there was any reference to the 'dry run' that she'd overheard Ivan talking about, but could see nothing. Ivan was a puzzle. On the one hand, his actions and words at the circus had been extremely suspicious. On the other, he'd rescued her from the Haunted House and been concerned for her welfare afterwards. So now she was confused. Was he an angel or a villain? It was hard to know.

On the walls of the office were dozens of photos of racehorses. Racehorses in the winner's circle, racehorses in photo finishes and in training. One caught her eye. It was a picture of Noble Warrior and his twin, Valiant, standing side by side. They were identical, peas in a pod. Laura could never have told one from the other except that Noble Warrior was wearing a halter with a brass Fleet Farm identification tag, and Valiant's halter had a silver V on the side. It was the silver V that made Laura's breath catch in her throat. She had a piece of it in an evidence bag in her room. It was the fragment she'd found the morning after they'd arrived.

Laura unpinned the photo and sat down to examine it closer.

The door opened and Mitch strode in. When he saw her with the logbook, he snatched it away. 'That, Miss, is private property. For the eyes of Fleet Farm staff only.'

Laura jumped up guiltily. 'I'm so sorry. I was just interested, that's all.'

'That's okay,' said Mitch, softening. 'But I'd appreciate it if you don't come in here unless you're with Kit or a staff member.'

Laura apologised profusely and gave him her word it wouldn't happen again.

'Think nothing of it,' Mitch said more kindly.

'Umm, I wondered if I could ask you a question?'

He checked his watch. 'Sure, fire away.'

'What is a dry run? Is it some kind of training term?'

He laughed. 'A training term? No, it's just an expression. Haven't you ever heard it? It means a rehearsal of some kind. A sort of trial run.'

The gears shifted in Laura's brain. A thought hovered but she couldn't quite grasp it.

The trainer picked up the photo on the table. 'Poor Warrior. No matter what he does in his life, no matter what he wins, he'll never escape the shadow of his twin.'

It was an odd comment, given that Noble Warrior was far more successful than Valiant and was hardly in danger of being overshadowed by him, but before Laura could ask anything else a dark look came over Mitch's face. Abruptly he tucked the book under his arm and jingled his keys to indicate that it was time for her to leave.

It was then that Laura saw her chance. 'How was the circus last night?' she asked casually. 'Did you enjoy it?'

He snorted. 'Circus? You couldn't get me to the circus if you paid me. No time for that kind of silliness at all. No, I spent the whole evening with Garth Longbrook, planning security arrangements for the Derby. Now, was that all?'

And with that he was gone, leaving Laura wondering yet again if her eyes had deceived her.

~ 18 ~

AT NOON, the lorry carrying Noble Warrior left Fleet Farm for Louisville, a journey of around an hour and a half, depending on traffic. Ken was in the driver's seat, accompanied by Kit and Tariq, who would keep an eye on the stallion throughout the journey, and Ivan, whose role was to watch for potential horse thieves.

Since there was barely room for four in the cab, Laura had to ride in convoy with security chief Garth Longbrook. He sported a fresh crew cut and was dressed in black commando-style clothing as if he was expecting a war. Prior to leaving the farm, she'd seen him tucking a gun into the glove compartment of his blue truck.

'Expecting an ambush?' Laura asked, tongue firmly in her cheek. She found it amusing how over-the-top the man was being.

He glowered at her. 'The mark of a true professional, kid, is always be prepared. Those criminals got past me once. It won't happen again. Not on my watch. Of course, it helps that Noble Warrior is travelling in an unmarked, rented lorry. The Fleet Farm lorry is still in the repair shop. The thieves smashed it up pretty badly.'

Laura tried to pluck up the courage to say something about the eureka moment she'd had in the night. Before she went to sleep, she'd been thinking about Mitch's reply to her question about the dry run. He'd said it referred to a rehearsal or a test run of some kind. Matt Walker frequently went to bed with a riddle in his head, because he claimed that the unconscious mind had an uncanny knack of solving it. Laura had done the same and the answer had astonished her.

She was now convinced that what she'd seen from her window on the first night had been a rehearsal for a crime. The thieves had practised stealing either Goldie or Noble Warrior. That had got her thinking about the whole subject of identical twins and another bit of the jigsaw had fallen into place.

What she didn't know was who to tell. She'd wanted to discuss it with Tariq but they hadn't known until the last second that they'd be travelling separately. She could risk ridicule and tell the security manager, but after the panic button fiasco of the first night she was nervous of incurring the wrath of the Wainwrights with another false alarm, and anyway what would it achieve? Garth had already torn a strip off her once for interfering. 'Spare me from amateur detectives,' he'd ranted. She didn't fancy going through it again.

For the first twenty-five minutes of the journey to Louisville, everything went smoothly. Garth tuned in to a country music station on the radio and unbent enough to ask Laura a little about St Ives. In turn he told her a couple of anecdotes from his years in the Navy. She warmed to him as he spoke and began to think she'd misjudged him.

'Mitch mentioned that he had dinner with you last night while you were going over the security arrangements,' she said, wondering if she'd catch him out in a lie.

However, Garth confirmed the story straight away. 'That's right, he did. I cooked him pepper steak, my speciality.' He braked suddenly. 'Hello, what's going on here?'

Ahead of them the lorry's exhaust was billowing black smoke. Its hazard lights came on and it spluttered slowly to a halt, only just managing to crawl into the car park of a roadside diner.

Garth sprang out of his truck and strode over to the lorry. Ken hopped down from the cab, followed by Ivan, Kit and then Tariq.

'Disaster, boss. The engine's packed up,' said Ken. 'I thought we could get a bit further if I nursed it along, but it quit on me.'

The security manager was livid. 'Of all the cursed luck. This is the last thing Noble Warrior needs.'

'You sink I should give Mitch a call?' Ivan suggested

worriedly. 'He can call rental company and maybe get us another lorry quick quick.'

'Good idea, Ivan,' Garth Longbrook said. 'Mitch will give them a blast and convey the urgency of the situation. Morons. That's the last time we use their firm.'

Ivan had to walk almost to the other end of the car park in order to get a phone signal. They watched him striding up and down, gesturing passionately. Finally, he returned. 'Mitch is bringing new lorry, but zere will be small delay. Maybe one hour.'

Garth made a noise that sounded like a dog growling, but a resigned shrug followed. 'Not a whole lot we can do about it, so let's make the best of it. You kids go with Ivan and Ken and have a bite to eat in the diner. I'll stay here and guard the lorry.'

Everyone turned to go except Laura. As soon as they were out of earshot, she said urgently to Garth: 'Please ask Ken to stay with you. This is how they're going to do it. This is how they're going to swap the horses.'

He was bewildered. 'Who? What horses? What are you talking about?'

'Noble Warrior and Valiant,' Laura said, her voice rising in agitation. 'They're going to exchange them. I'm not sure who's behind it, but I'm pretty sure they had a kind of dress rehearsal the night we got to Kentucky. The second lorry wasn't my imagination. Everything was real, including the chestnut horse they brought to replace Goldie or Noble Warrior. I'm not sure why they decided to change the venue. Maybe because you beefed up security.'

The security manager's head had started to sweat. He

ran a palm across his bristles. 'Miss Marlin, I'm a patient man, but you are trying my nerves severely. Since you and your friend arrived at Fleet Farm, there's been one catastrophe after another. Detectives are supposed to solve problems, not cause them. Now I'd strongly suggest that you join Tariq and Kit for lunch and keep your half-baked notions to yourself. I have a racehorse to protect.'

Ivan came trotting down the path from the diner. 'Everysing all right? I bring you burger and soda, Mr Longbrook.' He grinned at Laura. 'Come, Lapushka, leave the security to zee expert. Zere is no one better zan zis man.'

Ears burning, Laura followed him without another word. In the diner, a cheerful place with red-checked tablecloths, pine furniture and more country music, she exchanged glances with Tariq. He nudged her under the table. He was worried, too, she could tell. Neither of them believed that the breakdown was coincidental and both kept sneaking looks at the lorry, partially visible through the restaurant blinds. Garth Longbrook was leaning against it, smoking. Turning away, Laura scanned the menu and ordered a veggie burger, although the last thing she felt like doing was eating. Humiliation has a tendency to ruin the appetite.

Kit smiled kindly at her and offered her a taste of her malted shake. 'Don't pay any attention to Garth,' she said under her breath. 'Gramps didn't hire him for his personality.'

Before long, Laura was laughing in spite of herself. Ivan performed a couple of card tricks with the flourish of a born showman, and made dollar bills appear behind their ears and cents turn up under milkshakes. Ken's watch reappeared in the middle of his Caesar salad. He glared at Ivan as he fished it out and tried vainly to extract bits of Parmesan from the links of the silver strap.

'Remind me why we brought you along.'

Ivan winked at Laura and Kit, who were sitting side by side. 'Because Warrior is not going to win zee Derby without me,' he teased.

Laura joined the general laughter, but she felt uneasy. The warning given to her by her St Ives' neighbour, Mrs Crabtree, now seemed astonishingly insightful. The racing game was *a magnet for chancers, gamblers, criminals and dreamers,*' she'd said. *'The pretty horses, the rainbow jockey silks, the fancy hats of the ladies who go to watch, they're just the window dressing. Behind the scenes, there are tricks going on that would be the envy of any conjurer. Big money involved, you see. Wherever there are millions at stake, there'll be men trying to make even more and they'll do whatever it takes. Sleight of hand, smoke and mirrors, rabbits out of hats, you name it, they have it up their sleeves.'*

Laura looked over at Ivan, who was pulling a red silk bandana from his mouth. Was he the joker he made himself out to be, always smiling, always friendly, always ready to be helpful? There was plenty of evidence to support this. He had, after all, rescued her from the Haunted House. Or was he a chameleon? A man who hid a ruthless cunning beneath his carefree exterior? A man who pretended to be idle and useless, but was in fact honed to Superman fitness by his gruelling workouts in the quarry?

'Is everything all right, Laura?' Kit asked. 'You looked quite fierce for a moment.'

Laura forced a smile. 'Oh, I was just thinking about how I'm going to punish Tariq if he steals another one of my sweet potato fries.'

She glanced out of the window and was startled to see Garth Longbrook dashing across the lawn to the diner, clutching his stomach.

He burst through the door, eyes streaming and unfocused. His normally swarthy skin was blue-white. 'Something in the burger didn't agree me. Sorry folks. Lorry is arriving. Ken, can you deal—?' was all he managed to croak before bolting to the bathroom.

'Jeepers creepers,' said Ken, looking down at the remnants of his own burger. 'I hope we don't all get food poisoning.'

Before they could debate the matter further the replacement lorry pulled into the car park. Garth was forgotten as they rushed out to supervise the transfer of Noble Warrior in the face of an approaching storm. The wind had picked up and fat drops of rain were darkening the asphalt.

Mitch, the driver, jumped down from the lorry's cab and pressed a button to lower the back. 'Unbelievable,' he said. 'Last time we'll ever use Equine Hire. Know what their slogan is? Hire us! You can rely on us! I've threatened to sue if Noble Warrior doesn't win the Derby.

'Now Ken, I have an idea. Both of these lorries have rear doors that slide open as well as lower. Instead of dropping the ramps, we can open them on their hinges. If you get into the driver's seat and reverse so that the backs of the lorries are almost flush against one another, I'll press the buttons to slide both doors back. It'll be a breeze to then walk Warrior from one to the other. Save him going down one ramp and up the other, getting wet and being unnerved by all these cars zooming around. What do you think? How about it?'

'Genius,' said Ken. 'The less we stress the boy, the better. Let's get to it.' .

'Need any help, Mitch?' Kit offered hopefully.

'Thanks, Kit, but I think we should keep this simple. I can manage on my own.'

With that, he swung onto the back of the lorry containing Noble Warrior, while Ken edged the empty van nearer. He turned off the engine. There were a few anxious moments as hooves thudded and the lorries rocked beneath the weight of one ton of horse. Finally, Mitch called: 'All done.'

Ken started the engine again and moved forward cautiously. Laura joined the others at the rear of the vehicle. The chestnut stallion was safely installed. They could see his quarters and the tips of his ears. He was resting one foot.

'Would it be okay if I get in the lorry with him for a few minutes?' Tariq asked. 'I might be able to talk to him and relax him a bit.'

Mitch shook his head. He pressed the button that closed the door. 'No more delays. The best thing we can do for the horse is get him to the track ASAP and get him bedded down and comfortable.'

He clapped his hands together. 'Let's get the show on

the road, people. I'll wait here with the other lorry until the breakdown truck arrives. You head on to Louisville.' He glanced around. 'Wait a second, where's Longbrook?'

There was a croak and a green-gilled Garth limped around the side of the lorry. He raised a weak paw. 'Sorry again, folks. Glad you managed without me. I'm better but not yet firing on all cylinders. Ivan, would you mind driving me to Churchill Downs? I don't think I can be trusted to take the wheel. Laura, you go with Ken, Kit and Tariq in the main lorry. I'll need you all to help me keep an eye out for horse thieves. My guarding skills are somewhat compromised.'

As the lorry pulled out onto the rain-darkened highway, wipers swishing, an hour and twelve minutes behind schedule, Kit said anxiously: 'I hope this isn't a bad omen. Gramps is counting on us to get Noble Warrior to the track in one piece and in the best shape of his life. He's counting on us to help Warrior win the Derby.'

Laura said nothing. She had a sick feeling in her stomach and it had nothing to do with the burger she'd eaten.

'**THAT'S NOT** Noble Warrior!'

It was six a.m. on Saturday morning and the first time any of the children had seen the chestnut stallion since leaving Fleet Farm. The previous afternoon the hire company mechanic had called Blake Wainwright from his workshop to report that the lorry's engine had been sabotaged. Blake, who was already in Louisville with Christine, immediately rang Ken and instructed him to bring Kit, Laura and Tariq directly to the hotel before the lorry went on to Churchill Downs. All Kit's protests had been in vain.

'Sweetheart, do you know what this means?' her

grandfather had asked patiently. 'It means that somebody out there doesn't want Noble Warrior to run in the Derby. Until we know how serious the threat is, I don't want you kids anywhere near the stables. Calvin Redfern and the Ashworths will never forgive me if anything happens to Laura and Tariq. It's a great shame because I really wanted Tariq to spend some time with Noble Warrior after his journey. It's uncanny how the horse has taken to the boy. Loves him to bits.'

That evening, he and Christine took the children to a Mexican restaurant in atmospheric downtown Louisville. Against a backdrop of blooming desert cacti and sun-drenched markets, they ate tortillas and cheese enchiladas and sizzling fajitas served in skillets, washed down with an ice-cold sour cherry drink. It was fun, but for Laura and Tariq it didn't lessen the disappointment of not being allowed to help the chestnut stallion settle in for his first night at the historic track.

In the hotel room that she shared with Kit and Tariq, Laura slept badly. The luxurious surroundings couldn't erase Garth Longbrook's harsh words, which played over and over in her head. 'Detectives are supposed to *solve* problems, not cause them.'

He was right. She couldn't deny it. In the five days that she'd been in Kentucky, she hadn't come up with a solitary solution to the many mysteries that simmered below Fleet Farm's tranquil surface. Well, she had but they'd all fizzled away to nothing. She still didn't know where the wildcat phial had come from, or who'd planted it. The circus had been a dead end. She'd pinned nothing on Ivan. Even her encounter with Janet Rain now seemed remote, like a half forgotten nightmare.

Her only comfort was that Matt Walker had once or twice found himself in the same situation – all at sea and criticised for his supposedly far-fetched theories. Each time his gut instincts had proved as true as any compass.

Dawn was breaking before Laura fell into a coma-like sleep. Kit had woken her barely an hour later. As a result, she'd been groggy and uncommunicative over a breakfast of coffee and bagels.

It was not until they pulled off the highway and Laura saw the famed twin towers of Churchill Downs that she suddenly came to life. When she stepped out of the car and inhaled the misty morning air with its heady mix of horse and cut grass, some inexpressible emotion – part excitement, part terror – surged through her veins.

Five minutes later, she, like Blake Wainwright and Ken, was staring in mute astonishment at Tariq as he gestured towards the shining chestnut leaning over the stable door. The stallion's ears flickered back and forth, like little radio aerials. He wanted his breakfast and was trying to decide who was most likely to get it for him.

The Bengali boy was outwardly calm but his tone carried a note of urgency. 'This horse is not Noble Warrior,' he said again.

Ken gave a short laugh. 'You're kidding, right? Of course, it's Noble Warrior.'

Blake ruffled Tariq's hair. 'He's just fooling with us, aren't you son?'

Tariq regarded him with clear tiger's eyes. 'I wish I was,

sir, but I'm not. Believe me, this isn't Warrior. Look, usually he loves his left ear being rubbed. He goes all soppy. But this horse doesn't like his head being touched at all. He's nervous of us because he doesn't know us.'

Kit studied the stallion from several angles. 'Are you sure, Tariq? He might simply be a bit stressed from the journey.'

Laura said: 'Tariq is right, I know he is. Oh, it's not that I can tell the difference between the two horses. Obviously, I can't. But everything points to that. That's been their plan all along. They must have switched the horses when the lorry broke down. It didn't occur to me that it would have a false compartment. Mitch didn't move Noble Warrior at all. He simply shut the back of the old lorry and left the stallion in there. Then he opened the false compartment of the new lorry and let Warrior's replacement in, knowing that we'd believe he was Noble Warrior because it would never occur to anyone it wasn't. He also knew that there was only one person in the world who could tell that the new horse was actually Warrior's twin and that person wasn't in hospital. If I'm not mistaken, this horse is Valiant.'

Kit started to speak, but before she could get a word out Garth Longbrook rounded the corner with a smiling Mitch.

'Morning, folks,' said the security manager brightly, looking a great deal healthier than he had the previous day. 'Sorry we're a bit late, but we've been trying to track down Ivan who's not been seen since last night. How's our champion this morning?'

Blake ran his fingers through his white hair. 'Garth,

we have a bit of a dilemma. It's preposterous, I know, but Tariq has a theory that Noble Warrior has somehow been substituted and Laura here believes this stallion is actually Nathan Perry's horse, Valiant—'

'Rubbish!' Mitch said furiously, his mood changing from sunny to stormy in an instant. 'That's absolute baloney. I'd know Noble Warrior anywhere. This is insane. Churchill Downs has acres of CCTV and some of the best security anywhere in the world. As if anyone could steal Noble Warrior from here, much less substitute his twin. Who are you going to believe, me or some idiot children who've known the horse for less than five days?'

Blake Wainright's faded blue eyes flashed a warning. 'As I was saying, Laura has this hypothesis that the switch happened during the breakdown, but of course that can't possibly be true because you, Garth, were there throughout, as was Mitch who I'd trust with my life.'

Garth looked as if he might blow a gasket. Laura feared that if his gaze alighted on her, she might be incinerated. 'If I might speak frankly, sir,' he growled, 'these children have done nothing but cause chaos since the day you clapped eyes on them . . .'

'That's a total lie!' Kit burst out. 'First off, Gold Rush was stolen on *your* watch and we'd never have got him back had it not been for Laura, her uncle and Tariq. Second, I was almost killed and poor Red Bishop lost his life – also on your watch. I blamed myself and was devastated and utterly miserable for an entire year until Laura figured out that it wasn't an accident. Someone wanted Bishop out of the picture. This horse looks like Warrior to me, but if

Laura and Tariq believe he's been exchanged we should listen to them.'

'Garth, are you hearing this?' cried Blake. 'Could foul play have been involved in Bishop's demise? Did you have any idea of this?'

The security manager was apoplectic, but he took a deep breath and tried to get his temper under control. 'With the greatest of respect, sir, Laura Marlin fancies herself as an amateur detective and has an overactive imagination, and as Mitch pointed out this young boy knows next to nothing about horses.'

'That may be true,' said a voice from behind them, 'but he sure knows enough to tell identical stallions apart.'

They turned to see a slender, wiry youth with a mop of untidy brown hair and an open, friendly face. He was very pale. One of his legs was in plaster, his right wrist was bandaged and he was leaning on crutches.

'Ryan!' gasped Ken.

'Ryan, what the heck are you doing here?' demanded Blake. 'You should be in hospital.'

'Tariq is one hundred per cent correct,' Ryan told the assembled group. 'This is Valiant, not Noble Warrior. If you doubt my word, let's take him out onto the track. Valiant is barely fast enough to win a local handicap race. He couldn't match Noble Warrior's worst practice time. You need to face the fact that the horses have been exchanged.'

'Impossible,' Garth Longbrook said faintly, but his bluster had gone. His stricken expression reflected his inner turmoil. Despite his best preparations, another monumental disaster had taken place.

Blake Wainright looked defeated. 'Can you prove it? I mean, we can call the veterinarian and check his microchip – as you all know Nathan and I refuse to allow any of our horses to have the lip tattoos that are standard in racing – but in the meanwhile it would be helpful to know.'

'Yes, I can,' said Ryan. 'When Noble Warrior was a yearling, he got a fright one day when I was cleaning his feet and managed to cut himself. It was such a tiny scratch that I never mentioned it to anyone – didn't want to get into trouble, I guess – but afterwards it left a little scar. If this is Noble Warrior, he'll have white hairs in the shape of a W beneath his chest.'

Blake Wainright opened the stable door. 'Ken, could you do the honours?'

Running a soothing hand down the chestnut stallion's foreleg, the exercise rider crouched down and examined the area carefully. 'No W here.'

When he stood up, he was trembling. 'How could this happen? We were all there, weren't we Mitch? We were all watching.'

Everyone turned to the trainer. Laura opened her mouth to say, 'While we're on the subject of identical twins, this is not Mitch, it's his lookalike brother,' but she was too late. The man posing as Mitch was long gone.

Blake Wainright sank down onto a nearby stool. 'So that's it then. My best horse has been stolen and the trainer I'd counted on to help us win the Derby and save Fleet Farm may be the architect of our ruin.'

Kit ran to his side and put her arms around him. 'Don't despair, Gramps. We can fix this, I'm sure we can.'

He raised eyes in which all hope had been extinguished. '*How?* As you well know, I'm not one to give up without a fight, but our cause seems lost.'

Beside him, Garth Longbrook was a broken man.

'For starters,' Laura said. 'Mitch is *not* involved.' She held up a hand as Ken protested. Quickly, she related what she'd seen through the vent of the Haunted House – Ivan and the man she'd believed to be Mitch embracing like brothers.

'So what you're saying is that the man you saw at the circus wasn't Mitch at all – couldn't have been since he was enjoying a steak dinner with me?' Garth Longbrook asked.

For the first time since they'd met, he was staring at Laura with real respect and interest. 'Your theory is that the person you saw was in fact his identical twin, the no-good brother who is always borrowing money from him? That with Ivan working as the inside man, they hatched a plan to switch the horses and make thousands of dollars in illegal gambling? I suppose it was Ivan who slipped me some kind of poison at the diner yesterday, making it easier for them to get away with it?'

'I expect so,' said Laura, since he seemed to be addressing the question to her. 'If you send a search party, you'll probably find that the real Mitch is locked in a barn or store cupboard at Fleet Farm.'

'I suppose this means that Ivan and Mitch's brother were involved in Red Bishop's accident?' Kit said in disgust. 'They must be sick. Have they no conscience?'

Laura hated to disillusion her friend, but it was the obvious conclusion. She nodded. 'I'm sorry, Kit. Proving it might be difficult though. We still don't know where they got the wildcat potion from.'

Ken started as if he'd been pricked with something sharp. 'What are you talking about? What wildcat potion?'

Throughout the exchange, Tariq had been watching the exercise rider carefully. 'Remember that day when Honey bolted and almost hurtled off a cliff, nearly taking Laura and Kit with her? Well, we found a plastic phial in Honey's bridle that smelled like a lion or a tiger in a zoo. The same smell was on my jacket sleeve the first time I met Noble Warrior. That was why he attacked me. We figure that whoever did those things was also responsible for sending Red Bishop so mad with fear that he threw Kit and—'

'No!' Ken had tears in his eyes. 'I would never in a million years have harmed Bishop. I loved him. But it *is* my fault that Honey bolted with you, Laura.'

Blake jumped to his feet. 'I can't bear it. Not you as well, Ken. You're like a son to me.'

Ryan was aghast. 'How could you, Ken?'

Ken looked at his best friend, shame written all over his face. 'I did it for you, Ryan. I was so angry that Mr Wainright was bringing over a strange boy, some kid who knew nothing about racing, to look after Warrior that I wanted to scare him off. I put a few drops of this stuff called Horse Away on the sleeve of a jacket I planned to give Tariq. I knew Noble Warrior would react badly to it. After all the work you'd put into preparing him for the race, I didn't want someone else stealing your thunder while you were in hospital if Noble Warrior really did win the Derby.

'It didn't work, which says a lot about Tariq's courage and how good he is with horses, so I gave up. I knew it was a bad thing I'd done, because Tariq could easily have been injured and I felt guilty about it. Problem was, I forgot I'd left a phial of the Horse Away in the pocket of my jacket. Roberto called me and asked me to take a look at the fetlock of one of his mares. As I was about to open her stable door, I remembered the phial. I didn't want to upset the mare so I put the little bottle on a ledge near the tack room. When I came back for it, it was gone.'

'Why did that bother you?' asked Laura.

'Because I knew from what had happened with Noble Warrior how dangerous Horse Away could be if it fell into the wrong hands. I'd become convinced that the theft of Goldie was an inside job and that someone at Fleet Farm was on a mission to ruin Mr and Mrs Wainright. When the phial was taken and Honey went berserk, I was sure, especially when the quarry gate was left open and Laura and Kit were almost killed. Someone didn't want Laura asking difficult questions. I suspected Ivan, but I couldn't tell anyone without revealing my own guilty secret so I kept quiet. I've beaten myself up about it at least a thousand times since that day. I'll never forgive myself for being so stupid.'

A tear rolled down his face. 'I'm sorry, Kit and Laura

146

and Tariq. I can't say that enough. Mr Wainwright, I'm handing in my notice right now.'

'Don't even think of it, Ken,' snapped Blake. 'Where will I find another exercise rider as talented as you are? Yes, you've disgraced yourself and you're very fortunate that these girls didn't end up in A&E, but I've no doubt that you'll learn from this and be a kinder, more generous-spirited person.'

'You'd better be,' Ryan said pointedly, 'or you'll be finding yourself a new best friend. I, for one, am glad that Tariq is here.'

He put a hand on the younger boy's shoulder. 'Anyone who cares enough about Warrior to put his neck on the line the way Tariq did this morning can be my assistant and share my thunder any time.'

'You've told the truth and you're genuinely sorry,' Kit told Ken. 'That's good enough for me.'

'And me,' Laura responded with feeling. 'Just one thing. The wildcat potion – this Horse Away – where did you get it?'

'Ivan brought a big tub of it to the farm just over a year ago,' Ken told her. 'He claimed that a friend of his – some zoo owner in Eastern Europe – was trying to patent it. Said it was real useful when it came to keeping horses away from poisonous weeds or stallions from breaking through fences.'

'Meanwhile, he and Mitch's evil brother really wanted to use it to terrify Red Bishop and stop him from winning the Derby,' Kit said furiously. 'Only their plan backfired when Gramps decided that I should be the one to exercise

Bishop. That's why 'Mitch' got so angry. It wasn't Mitch at all, it was his brother. It suddenly came home to him that if Bishop went crazy, they might have *my* death or broken bones on their conscience as well.'

Her grandfather looked as if he'd had all the shocks he could handle for one day. 'So it's a tale of twins, one fast and one slow, one good and one wicked beyond imagining. How did you guess that Mitch had an identical twin, Laura?'

'It was something Mitch said. He commented that no matter what Noble Warrior did in his life, no matter what he won, he'd never escape the shadow of his twin. Since I'm pretty sure that the last thing on Warrior's mind is his brother, it made me think that he might be talking about himself. It was Mitch who lived in someone's shadow.'

Blake was exhausted. The strain of the past few weeks showed in the sharp-etched lines on his kind face. 'Will we ever see Noble Warrior again, Garth, or do you think they've already spirited him across the Atlantic like the men who stole Goldie?'

A ghost of a grin crossed the security manager's face. He turned to the children. 'If you were me, where would you start looking, Laura Marlin? Any suggestions?'

She smiled back. 'I'd begin with Nathan Perry's farm. I have a feeling that you'll find Noble Warrior standing in Valiant's stall wearing a halter with a broken silver V on it.'

His mouth dropped open. 'How could you possibly know . . . ? Oh never mind. When this is over, I want a few private investigator tips from you. I'm also going to be buying a whole stack of Matt Walker novels.'

He extended his hand first to Laura, then to Tariq. 'I apologise unreservedly for calling you an amateur, Laura. You could run rings around most professionals, including me. And, Tariq, thanks to you and Ryan we might yet be in with a chance to enter a horse in the Derby. Now if you'll excuse me, I have a racehorse to rescue.'

'HEY, GUYS, what do you think? Do I pass muster?' asked Kit, emerging from the hotel bathroom. Tariq, sprawled on the bed in a borrowed suit, gave a teasing whistle, but Laura was momentarily speechless. Gone was their farm kid friend with the wild hair, ripped jeans and worn boots. In her place was a dazzling young woman in a figure-hugging white dress patterned with red roses. On her head was a navy blue hat with a wide brim and a matching white and rose scarf twisted around it. She wore white Roman sandals and had painted her toenails crimson.

'You look sensational,' Laura said in awe. 'Like a supermodel.'

Kit giggled and hugged her. 'Until tomorrow morning, when I'll put on my cowboy boots and jeans again and be glad to do it. But today is a special occasion. Everyone in Kentucky dresses up. You look very pretty yourself by the way. And Tariq is going to stop traffic in that suit. Now are you ready for Derby Day?'

When they descended to the lobby to meet the Wainrights, Laura saw what Kit meant. It was crammed with racegoers dressed in their finery, some of it elegant, some of it eye-popping and some of it – Tariq pointed out a woman who appeared to have a bowl crammed with tropical fruit on her head – plain bizarre.

There was a carnival atmosphere. A milliner, with a stall displaying pillbox hats and others adorned with feathers or netting, strutted like a peacock as he marketed his wares. There were tables stacked high with Kentucky Derby hats, T-shirts and mugs. Screened by a wall of lilies and roses, diners tucked into white egg omelettes and two Southern favourites – grits, a kind of porridge topped with melted cheese, and biscuits, which to Laura looked exactly like scones. They weren't served with clotted cream and strawberry jam as was customary in St Ives, but with a creamy pork gravy. Laura, who was a vegetarian, found this incomprehensible.

Outside, they joined the long lines of people streaming down the road to the racetrack. 'The traffic's so bad on Derby Day, anyone who can walks,' Christine explained. 'For the police and Churchill Downs officials, it's a huge operation. During Derby week, there are some twelve thousand employees taking care of around a hundred and seventy thousand visitors and the stables are full to bursting. Fourteen hundred horses are kept in the forty-eight barns.'

'Racing people are superstitious, so there's no barn thirteen,' added Kit with a laugh.

As the twin spires came into view, framed against a crisp blue sky, Laura suspected that everyone in their party was all saying the same silent prayer. After everything that has blighted the fortunes of Fleet Farm, please let it be our day today. She knew too that the Wainrights and Kit were still filled with wonder that they were at Churchill Downs at all and in with a chance.

Tariq had already been to the stables with Ryan and Ken that morning and reported that Noble Warrior was in fine fettle and none the worse for wear after his adventure. 'He's all cocky and pleased with himself, as if he's been on a particularly good holiday. You'd never think that he'd been abducted by criminals.'

Tariq and Laura were the heroes of the hour because Tariq had spotted that the horses had been switched, and Laura's hunch had proved correct. When Garth Longbrook and the police had torn through the gates of Nathan Perry's farm the previous day, they'd found Noble Warrior – identified via his microchip by the racing authorities – happily munching hay in Valiant's stall. As Laura had predicted, he'd been wearing Valiant's halter with the broken silver V.

It subsequently turned out that at least two of Nathan's grooms had been in on the fraud and had long criminal records. There was also evidence to suggest that they'd been involved in the plot to harm Red Bishop, which meant that the case against Blake Wainright would be dropped immediately. Much of the money he'd paid out in legal costs would be returned to him. Nathan Perry was said to be mortified and had already called Blake with a stammered but very sincere apology.

Mitch had been discovered locked in the bathroom of his cottage. He'd yelled himself almost hoarse, but as he resided at the far end of the farm, nobody had heard him. Since he was supposed to be in Louisville, no one had thought to look for him either. When he found that his worst fears had been realised and that his own brother had tried to destroy another Derby favourite, he was devastated. He'd wanted to resign on the spot, but Blake had persuaded him to come to Churchill Downs and do his best to get Noble Warrior ready for the race. They'd talk about his future after that.

Laura had called home to tell Calvin Redfern a carefully worded version of the drama before he read it in the newspapers, but there'd been no reply at number 28 Ocean View Terrace. She kept checking her mobile to see if he'd left a message, but there was nothing. She didn't worry. If he was on a job pursuing fishermen with illegal catches, he could be out most of the night.

At the Churchill Downs' turnstiles, they were whisked through, with many of those queuing for tickets recognising the Wainrights and wishing them luck. The first races were already underway. Some of the most exquisite horses Laura had ever laid eyes upon were being led around the Paddock.

As graceful as panthers and dainty as ballet dancers, they circled before the watching crowd, champing at the chain shanks used by some trainers to keep their horses under control. In Laura's opinion, it was far too harsh a measure for such sensitive beasts. An overhead screen broadcast the current race live.

Some of those watching rushed away to place their bets before the horses were led out onto the track. Laura could not get over the amount of money that seemed to be changing hands at the tote, the racecourse betting facility, where rows of cashiers were ringing up or dishing out cash. While the Wainwrights went to the Jockey Room to talk to the jockey who'd be riding Noble Warrior that afternoon, Kit gave Tariq and Laura a guided tour of the main building.

Each of the six levels was awash with people in glamorous outfits holding glasses of champagne. They moved between the buffet counters, the bar and the betting counters. Floor four was known as Millionaire's Row. On the stairwell outside the palatial rooms was a glass sculpture of Churchill Downs with four hundred glass figurines of jockeys, horses and spectators, perfect in every detail.

As the friends ascended so did the wealth. The people in the Finish Line suites had their own special room with their own personal waiters and they could put up the colourful silks worn by their chosen jockey. The people with the most money occupied the Gold Rooms on Floor Two and Six. Kit told Laura that these men and women would think nothing of putting on a single horse the kind of cash that would buy a house.

'Where does all this money go?' asked Laura. 'Is it kept in some sort of vault?'

'It goes down to the Money Room beneath the grandstand. It's heavily guarded. You'd have more chance of getting into The White House.'

Laura could tell that Tariq, who came from a desperately poor background in Bangladesh, was uncomfortable with such ostentatious displays of extravagance. They were both happier when Kit took them into the media centre, where the racing reporters were pounding away at their keyboards or out on the balcony, watching the horses cross the finish line on the track below.

They were an amiable bunch, passing the time between deadlines with banter and chocolate chip cookies. A couple of them smiled at the children, but most paid no attention to the trio at all. They'd be kicking themselves later in the day when the news broke about the dramatic raid on Nathan Perry's farm and rescue of Noble Warrior and it hit them that they'd unknowingly had under their noses the three key players in the biggest racing scandal of the year.

For now, however, they were oblivious.

As Kit pushed open the balcony doors of the media centre, the roar of the crowd came at them like a wave. The air practically crackled with anticipation. Each race was preceded by a trumpet blast known as the Call to the Post. Pony Boys, who were not boys at all but men and women on trusty steeds, accompanied the racehorses and their jockeys to the starting gates. They were outriders. Their job was to help any rider battling with an excitable mount, or to pick up loose horses after falls.

Tariq leaned over the rails, enraptured, as a line of horses burst from the gates on the far side of the track. On the huge screen behind the finish line, they could see them travelling at electrifying speed round the track. Finally they came into view and a jockey in yellow urged a powerful grey named Wanderlust to victory.

It was while Tariq was hanging over the side, trying to see the winner being presented with the trophy that Laura heard him draw a startled breath.

'What is it?' She knew immediately that something was wrong.

He pointed. 'At the bottom of the grandstand, next to the track rail. See those people dressed in stars and stripes, like an American flag. The woman beside them wearing black, like a widow.'

Laura shielded her eyes from the sun. 'Janet Rain!'

'The monster woman!' cried Kit. 'Where? Oh, I see her. She doesn't look like a kidnapper who enjoys torturing children. She looks like someone who just stepped from the pages of *Vogue*. Are you sure it's the same person?'

Their faces told her everything she needed to know. 'Got it. Well, what do you want to do about it? Confront her? Call the cops?'

In the split second it took for Laura to reply, Janet Rain had gone, melting into the crowd.

Tariq's eyes met Laura's. 'As we came through the turnstiles this morning I thought I saw Ivan on the other side of the glass. I wasn't sure because he looked so different. His long blond hair seemed to have been cut short and dyed black. The sun was shining on the glass, which made it difficult to see, and when we went through he was gone. I didn't want to say anything in case I'd made a mistake.'

Laura turned to Kit. 'When Goldie was stolen, was there anything left behind in the Fleet Farm lorry? Any clue. Maybe something a bit surprising.'

Kit shook her head. 'Nothing. Not a fingerprint, not a trace of DNA. It was as if a ghost had taken him. Oh, wait. After the detectives had gone, Ken found a playing card wedged behind a bench, a Joker, but we figured that it was probably one of Ivan's. You know how he's always doing card tricks.'

Laura went quite still. 'Of course! How obvious. How could I not have figured that out sooner? The Joker might have belonged to Ivan, but if it did it's because he's a member of the Straight A gang. The Joker is their calling card. It's their way of laughing at the police. They leave it when they think they've got away with something.'

She took a deep breath. 'So it was them all along. They've been behind everything. Ivan and Mitch, and the father and son arrested for stealing Goldie in the UK, they're all linked to the Straight A's. And now at least two of the gang are here at the Kentucky Derby'

'I don't understand,' said Kit. 'What does this mean?'

'It means that they're up to something,' replied Laura darkly, 'and whatever it is, it's going to be huge.'

~ 21 ~

'WE WARNED YOU, *Laura Marlin* . . .'

The words brushed the back of Laura's neck like an ill wind as she stood in a shadowy corridor near the Paddock. She was waiting for Kit who was attempting to wash a coffee stain out of her dress in the bathroom. At the time, Laura was texting her uncle yet again. He wasn't fond of the phone, but he was as reliable as snow in winter when it came to returning messages. The fact that he'd been silent for nearly twenty-four hours was worrying her.

For that reason, her reactions were slower than normal. Before she could blink Janet Rain had a grip on her like an anaconda crushing a mouse. 'You thought you could escape me, Laura Marlin, didn't you? Well, you thought wrong. No one ever escapes Janet Rain. If that imbecile, Ivan, had been quicker off the mark in the Haunted House, he'd have got to you before your boyfriend turned up and you'd have joined the ranks of the disappeared.'

As Janet swooped, her hand moving in to cover Laura's mouth, Laura let out a piercing scream. Janet gave a winded gasp and her grip abruptly loosened.

'Stay away from her, you . . . you black widow spider,' yelled Kit, who had karate-kicked Janet in the solar plexus. 'Security! Somebody please help us! *HELP!* Fire! FIRE!'

In the ensuing chaos, when a fire crew burst from nowhere, accompanied by several burly crowd members, and Kit had to explain about a hundred times that she'd only screamed fire because it was an emergency and not because the grandstand was actually burning to the ground, Janet Rain fled.

The firemen were angry because their time had been wasted. In Laura's opinion, they were mostly annoyed because two shrieking girls had dragged them away from the television screens showing the latest race, but she couldn't exactly say that. And anyway, they weren't the only people in a huff.

The Churchill Downs' officials were in a flat spin because they were worried that a child abductor was on the loose. And the racegoers were furious because a race was delayed without explanation. As if that wasn't bad enough, a couple of pompous cops made fun of Laura when she tried to tell them that a female member of the world's most notorious gang was at the Derby and up to no good.

'Let's put it this way, kid, she's not alone,' one laughed.

'Somehow we've got to keep this from Grandma and Gramps,' Kit whispered to Laura as they tried to slip away from the throng. 'Promise me, you won't say anything. They're so overjoyed to be here, and so looking forward to seeing Noble Warrior run, that I can't bear to upset them. Besides, if Gramps has any more shocks this week, he'll have a heart attack.'

'But Janet Rain needs to be stopped,' Laura told her. 'If you hadn't turned out to be a martial arts expert, who knows what would have happened to me. They're big fans of chloroform, the Straight A's. One sniff of that stuff and you're out stone cold and you don't know a thing until you wake up hours later with a headache.'

'I know, but please wait until after the race,' implored Kit. 'In an hour's time, I'll do whatever you want me to. I'll shout it from the roof of the grandstand. Just promise me you won't do anything till then. What difference is sixty minutes going to make?'

You have no idea how much difference an hour can make with the Straight A's is what Laura wanted to say. But she refused to ruin this long-awaited moment for the Wainrights with her hunches and flights of fancy. She'd been wrong many times before. Why not now?

She gave Kit a big smile as they turned to go. 'I promise.'

'Not so fast,' barked the cop. 'Where are your parents? We need to have a serious talk.'

Kit said politely but firmly: 'We're with my grandparents,

but I really don't think it's a good idea to disturb them right now, Officer.'

He drew himself up to his full height, which wasn't very high. 'And why is that?'

'Because,' Kit told him, 'that's our horse, Noble Warrior, being led into the Paddock as we speak, and my Gramps has waited all year for this special moment. Besides, I may have exaggerated a teeny weeny bit about the emergency. You see, this woman we don't like was being horrible to Laura and it was the only way we could think of to get rid of her.'

The other cop shaded his eyes. 'Noble Warrior? Isn't he the favourite to snatch the Derby from Kindred Spirit?'

Kit beamed with pride. 'That's right. And he will win too.'

The man looked at his partner. 'Is there any law against betting in uniform?'

'If there is, I've forgotten it.'

'Okay, girls, thanks for the tip. Give your Grandma and Gramps our best for the Derby. Oh, and remember, never ever waste police time. While you're making up stories, real criminals could be getting away with murder.'

'Yes, Officer, sorry, Officer,' giggled Kit. She looped her arm through Laura's. 'Let's go and see Noble Warrior run.'

Laura had never felt prouder of anyone in her life than she did watching her best friend lead Noble Warrior around the Paddock, watched by millions around the world. Tariq grinned at her as he passed and her heart contracted. To see him so happy made everything worth it. She'd go through all of it again – well, maybe not the death-defying ride on Honey – just to make him smile.

Noble Warrior looked magnificent. His muscles rippled beneath his fiery coat and, despite his smallness, he carried himself regally and held his head high. To Laura, he seemed more than a match for his main rivals – the strapping bay, Kindred Spirit, and a tall, excitable grey, Speed Merchant.

'The media has those two as his biggest threats,' Blake explained to Laura, 'but there are a couple of outsiders I fear. Avatar and Comic Timing.'

'Don't forget Monsoon,' Ryan put in, enviously watching Tariq parade Noble Warrior around the Paddock. Tariq had fully expected Ryan to do it himself, but Ryan had refused. 'Nobody wants to see someone on crutches hobbling around the Paddock, trying to hang on to a keyed-up stallion. This is Warrior's moment to shine. And yours, for that matter.'

'In other words,' Kit was telling Laura, 'it's an open field. That's what makes the Derby so great, anyone can win.'

Across the Paddock, Garth Longbrook was watching Noble Warrior's every move, flanked by two plainclothes' detectives. Pride had caused him to make many mistakes over the past few months, but he'd been well and truly humbled, and Laura was sure that in the future there'd be no better head of security in any racing stable.

'You were right about what happened on the first night

you arrived,' he'd told her earlier that morning. 'There *was* a second lorry. Ivan and the men from Nathan Perry's farm rehearsed unloading Valiant, switching him over, and then driving away again, all before the CCTV camera clicked to the barn. It took longer than they expected so that's when they made the decision to switch the horses while Warrior was in transit. There was a false compartment, exactly as you'd surmised.'

Kit nudged Laura. 'Don't you just love the racing saddles? They're feather-light, like children's toys. For most races, the declared weight of the jockey – that's his or her weight and the saddle – has to be under a hundred and twenty pounds. If I become a jockey, I'll have to stop eating Anita's waffles.'

A photographer interrupted them. 'Excuse me, ma'am, sir,' he said to Christine and Blake. 'Would you mind if I took a photo of the two of you with your pretty granddaughter? It's for the society page of the local paper.'

Kit rolled her eyes at Laura as they were led away. 'Back in a sec.'

Laura had been standing on her own for less than a minute when her neighbour tapped her on the shoulder. 'Miss, a young man just slipped a note into your pocket.'

The goosebumps stood up on Laura's arms. 'What man?'

But whoever it was had gone. Laura scanned the crowds for Janet or Ivan, but could see neither. Cautiously, she put her hand in her pocket. It wasn't a note but a playing card. A malevolent Joker, grinning fiendishly.

Her blood ran cold. Whatever the Straight A's were

planning was about to happen. With minutes to go until the Kentucky Derby, what else could it be but the race. They must be planning to rig it somehow.

She looked over at Kit and her grandparents, posing and laughing for the photographer, and at Noble Warrior, prancing beside Tariq. She'd promised Kit that she wouldn't spoil this moment for them. She had no intention of going back on her word.

Suddenly Laura felt very alone. If only her uncle was here. He would know what to do. He would take charge. She checked her phone for the hundredth time. No message. Where was he?

And then, like a mirage, she saw him. He was striding through the crowds, instantly recognisable, not because his grey suit was plain in comparison to the resplendent outfits surrounding him, but because he, like Noble Warrior, carried himself in a way that made him stand out from the crowd.

He swept Laura off her feet and swung her round until she was dizzy and laughing. 'Sorry not to call, but I wanted to surprise you,' he said when he set her down. I did talk to Blake yesterday and I gather that you and Tariq have been very busy. In fact, I gather that if it weren't for the two of you, Noble Warrior would not be running in the Kentucky Derby.'

Laura looked sheepish. 'We did do our best to stay out of trouble, it's just that . . .'

He grinned. 'Don't tell me, it's just that mysteries kept needing to be solved.'

'In a way.'

The horses' girths were being tightened and the jockeys – tiny men and women with leathery skin, wearing colourful silk jerseys – were being hoisted into the saddle. They were so strong they looked bionic. The Wainright's jockey, wearing an ultramarine blue and white silk jersey, was hovering nervously beside Noble Warrior.

Calvin Redfern's face was suddenly serious. 'Laura, to be honest, I'm not only here for pleasure. I'm here because the police have had a tip-off that the Straight A's are planning something at the Derby. Our only problem is that we haven't a clue what it is, but we imagine it's something to do with the race itself.'

It was then that Laura a light bulb moment. She had a flashback of Ivan doing his sprint training in the heat of the day.

'It's not the race,' she cried. 'It's all been an elaborate smokescreen. Maybe not the theft of Goldie, but the swapping of Noble Warrior, the hints that somebody somewhere was going to try to fix the race. They were red herrings – distractions.'

'Distractions from what? That's what police intelligence has failed to discover.'

'It's not the horses that they're after,' Laura told him. 'It's the money. You once said to me that the Straight A's don't bother themselves with thousands. They're interested in millions or even billions. I think they're planning to raid the Money Room during the two minutes that the Derby is being run, when everyone's attention – including the guards – is likely to be on the race.'

Her uncle's eyes widened. 'Of course, that's it. How

could we have been so blind? They're after the money. Every cent of it.'

He pulled a radio from his pocket. 'Attention all units. Stand by for orders.'

Laura smothered a grin. Her uncle had been in Kentucky a matter of hours and yet he had already taken command. After the nail-biting tension of the past few days, it was nice to hand the reins of the investigation to someone else.

Kit came rushing up. 'Is everything all right?' she demanded, looking suspiciously at Calvin Redfern.

'It will be now,' Laura assured her. 'Uncle Calvin, this is my friend, Kit. Kit, this is my uncle, Calvin Redfern. Uncle Calvin, please let me come with you.'

He gave her a quick squeeze. 'No, Laura, you've done more than enough and this could get ugly. Go and enjoy the race with your friends. Kit, it's a pleasure to meet you, albeit briefly. The very best of luck to Noble Warrior.'

And with that he was gone.

~ 22 ~

LAURA BLINKED AS a dozen cameras clicked and whirred, and flashbulbs popped once again. 'Over here, please. Big smile, ma'am! Kit, how about a kiss on the nose for Noble Warrior? Oh, that's adorable. Again, if you wouldn't mind?'

If there hadn't been a wall of photographers in front of her, and cameras beaming her image into millions of homes across the globe, Laura would have had to pinch herself. At Sylvan Meadows Children's Home she'd spent hundreds of hours dreaming of a time when she might travel to exotic places and have adventures, but never in her wildest imaginings did she think that on the day she'd

167

helped foil one of the most audacious robberies in racing history, she'd also be in the Winner's Circle with the stallion who'd swept all before him in the Kentucky Derby.

Not that Noble Warrior hadn't given them a heart attack or two. The instant before the starting gate had opened, the jockey in the adjacent stall sneezed. Whether it was because the red stallion momentarily lost concentration or because he got a fright, he broke last. Within seconds, he'd been left behind and a gap had opened up between him and the rest of the field.

'What a disaster,' cried Blake.

'Unbelievable,' Christine said despairingly. 'That's it. The race is over before it's begun.'

'The race isn't over until it's over with Noble Warrior,' Ken comforted her. 'Nothing he hates more than seeing the quarters of the horse in front of him. Nothing he likes more than a challenge. Look closely. You can see him gathering himself. Now watch him go.'

'Ken's right,' Mitch agreed. 'Warrior has the heart of a lion. He's inherited all Goldie's courage and more. He'll never give up.'

Laura strained her eyes. She wanted to see every detail of the horses thundering down the track. They powered towards her, dirt spraying from beneath their mighty hooves, nostrils flaring, veins popping, one with his tongue hanging out of the side of his mouth.

The roar of the crowd was like nothing she'd ever heard. It filled her ears. The air crackled with electricity. Elegant women were jumping up and down in their stilettos. Men in thousand dollar silk suits were screaming their favourites' names like teenagers at a pop concert.

'Come on, Speed Merchant!'

'You can do it, Kindred Spirit!'

'Show them who's boss, Avatar!'

And the Noble Warrior fans:

'Oh no!'

'This is a tragedy.'

'Oh, dear.'

Their partners were berating them: 'Didn't I tell you to put money on Speed Merchant? Didn't I? But you never listen. As if that little red horse is any match for him.'

Speed Merchant and an outsider called Tearaway were dominating the race, burning up the track, when Noble Warrior suddenly seemed to find an extra gear. He closed the gap and began to streak through the field.

'Noble Warrior is making a move,' the commentator yelled excitedly. 'My goodness, they don't call him the Pocket Rocket for nothing. But it may not be enough. Speed Merchant has a commanding lead and now Avatar is on the attack. Kindred Spirit is being pulled up by his jockey. His saddle seems to have slipped. Look at Warrior go, though. He is flying. It's hard to believe a horse so small can take a stride that comes close to matching Man o' War's legendary gallop, but he does.'

'Go Warrior!' screamed Kit.

Laura felt as if her heart might burst out of her chest with excitement. Tariq was jumping up and down as if he was on a trampoline, and Ryan was waving a crutch in the air.

'I don't believe it,' cried the commentator. 'He's ridden

down Speed Merchant and Tearaway, both flagging, and he's going after Avatar. Can he do it? Oh my word, he has, and by a neck. It's Noble Warrior from Avatar and Comic Timing, with Speed Merchant back in fourth place. Ladies and Gentlemen, Noble Warrior, firstborn son of the legendary Gold Rush, wins the Kentucky Derby in heroic style.'

In the grandstand, everyone seemed to be in tears, including Laura. Kit grabbed her and Tariq and the three of them danced around in an ecstatic circle. Christine and Blake were hugging each other. Ken and Ryan were already on their way headed down to the track to wait for Noble Warrior.

Shortly afterwards Laura found herself in the Winner's Circle in front of the world's press and racing audiences from Cornwall to China. Tariq, Ryan, Ken and Laura stood on one side of Noble Warrior, while Kit, her grandparents, Garth Longbrook and the jockey beamed on the other. Mitch had hung back at first, still gutted that his own brother had been involved in a deception that had almost cost them the race, but Christine insisted he join them.

'You're your own person, Mitch,' she told him. 'You are not your brother. It's because of your brilliant training that Warrior was able to win. That's what you need to remember.'

Beside her, the red stallion arched his neck and preened and posed. Draped around his neck was the garland of crimson roses.

Despite the joy of the occasion, Laura had a knot in her stomach. Where was her uncle? Was he safe? She was terrified that he'd be hurt trying to stop the Straight A's. During his years as a detective, he'd had plenty of experience in dealing with the gang, but there was no end to their cunning and in recent months they'd gone to enormous lengths to try to take revenge on him. Each time he – with the help of Laura, Tariq and some unlikely friends – outwitted them, they became angrier and more intent on vengeance.

'That's enough guys,' said the media officer, holding up his hand to the photographers like a traffic policemen. 'The scribes need to hear the story too. We're going to escort the Wainrights up to the media centre.'

He turned to Blake. 'I believe that you have quite a tale to tell, sir. One of stolen stallions and a devilish plot by an identical twin to switch identical twins. As incredible as that is, another story is breaking which might rival it for front page news. Would you believe that while the Derby was being run, a gang of international thieves tried to rob the Money Room. They didn't succeed because the cops had received a tip-off. Several of these gangsters are being led away in handcuffs as we speak. I caught a glimpse as I dashed down here. One looked quite familiar. You didn't have a boy called Ivan working for you, did you?'

As the Wainwrights were led away, Laura turned her phone on. There were two messages. The first was a text from her uncle.

Hey Laura, thanks to you, we caught 'em red-handed. Put it this way, you'll not be hearing from Ms Rain ever again.

Have some loose ends to tie up, but will see you at Fleet Farm tonight. Love, Uncle C x

Her mobile beeped again. This time it was from an unknown sender.

Bravo, Laura Marlin! You are a worthy adversary. Until we meet again . . . Mr A

It was a glorious afternoon, but Laura suddenly felt chilled to the bone. The fact that the elusive head of the Straight A's, leader of one of the world's most notorious criminal empires, knew her phone number was, frankly, chilling. *'Until we meet again . . . ?'* She didn't even want to think about what that meant.

She glanced around quickly. Somehow she knew beyond doubt that he was here at the Derby, watching her. She refused to show she was scared. 'Sooner or later, we'll catch up with you,' she mouthed silently. 'Sooner or later, justice will be done.'

'Why are you looking so serious?' demanded Kit, extricating herself from a crowd of well-wishers and putting an arm around Laura's shoulders. 'We have so much to celebrate. As soon as Grandma and Gramps are done with the media, we're going back to Fleet Farm and having a dinner party with every treat you can think of.

'Oh, I'm so happy that you stepped into our lives, Laura Marlin. It's because of you and Tariq that Goldie is safe, that Warrior had a chance to win the Derby and that Fleet Farm will now always belong to Grandma and Gramps.

And that's not all. You've also given me back my life. I can ride again. I can dream again. That's wonderful, but it's not the best part. The best part is that I feel as if I've gained a friendship that will last forever. I feel . . . I hope you don't mind me saying this . . . as if I have a sister and brother in you and Tariq.'

'That's cool with me,' Tariq said with a laugh, as he came over to join them. Someone had put one of Warrior's red roses in the buttonhole of his suit. 'I feel the same way about you.'

'And so do I,' Laura agreed heartily. 'Now, you mentioned something about a celebration . . . '

Author's Note

When I was a child in Africa, my father spent several years working for Thomas Beattie, a farmer who was a highly successful racehorse owner. They'd become friends when Dad rode for him as an amateur jockey, and as a consequence of the thrilling stories they told and my daily encounters with the magnificent thoroughbreds that grazed in fields around our house, I became captivated by horse racing.

The highlight of the trip I made to the US to research this book – apart, obviously, from going to the Kentucky Derby – was visiting the Kentucky Horse Park, where I saw the statues of Man o' War and Secretariat, two of the greatest racehorses of all time. I also visited some of the Lexington farms. It was there that I met two stallions worth $80 million and $65 million. They lived in palatial comfort in a sort of house. When we drove up, one was looking out of the window.

For champions like Noble Warrior and Goldie, the life of a racehorse is very good indeed, but they are in a tiny minority. As Laura discovered, racing has a dark side. Horses are not fully grown until they are eight years old, which is why most riding horses do not begin their training until they are three or four. Racehorses, on the other hand, are routinely 'started' at eighteen months and raced at two years old. They are babies being pushed to their physical and mental limits.

Because their bones are not yet fully developed, these young horses frequently pull ligaments, strain tendons or fracture limbs. It's estimated that in North America alone up to eight hundred horses a year die from injuries sustained while racing. Even if they do stay fit, their fate depends on their performances. Those that don't make the grade are seldom lucky enough to go to kind homes, racehorse retirement homes or sanctuaries. The majority are sold to owners who can't handle them, euthanised, sent to slaughterhouses to be turned into pet food, or shipped abroad to countries to be sold as horse meat.

Racing is expensive. One survey of the Australian racing industry showed that fewer than ten per cent of racehorses make a profit for their owners. That means that some unscrupulous owners force their horses to run even when injured, masking the pain with things like cobra venom or cone snail venom. Anyone who read *Kidnap in the Caribbean* will remember the latter as one of the deadliest toxins on earth. Exhausted horses are sometimes forced on by jockeys who can whip them as many as thirty times in a race.

That said, it's important to remember that across the world there are numerous trainers, owners and jockeys who love the horses in their care and do their very best to treat them with respect and compassion. And there's no doubt that the horses who are treated right love to run. Go to YouTube and watch Australian wonder horse, Black Orchid, in action. She lives to race. Or see the movie,

Secretariat. The red stallion loved to run so much that when he finished a race he was often halfway round the track before his jockey could pull him up.

If you enjoy watching horses compete in any sport, whether it be racing, showjumping or eventing, try to do your part to ensure that the horses have the life they deserve. Sponsor charities like World Horse Welfare, or hold cake or car boot sales to help support racehorse retirement homes or sanctuaries. Whether or not they're champions, every horse is precious.

Lauren St John,
London
2012

If you've enjoyed *Kentucky Thriller* you'll also love Lauren St John's other Laura Marlin Mysteries.

Dead Man's Cove

'What I want,' Laura declared, 'is to have a life packed with excitement like some of the characters in my books.'

Orphaned Laura is sent to live with her uncle in Cornwall, convinced that a life of adventure is hers at last. But everywhere she turns she's confronted with mysteries. Is Tariq, the shopkeeper's silent son, a friend or an enemy? Why does her uncle seem intent on erasing his own past? And why is everyone so afraid of Dead Man's Cove?

Kidnap in the Caribbean

'We've bought you here to teach you a lesson you'll never forget, Laura Marlin . . .'

Laura Marlin has no idea that her dream holiday to the Caribbean might cost her and everyone she loves their lives.

But almost as soon as they board the luxury cruise ship mysteries begin to pile up and sinister events spiral out of control.

When her uncle disappears, Laura, her best friend Tariq, and beloved husky Skye must play a deadly game with their enemies. Thousands of miles from home, face to face with pirates, a volcano and hungry sharks, their best hope of survival is the advice of a fictional detective and the help of disaster-prone Jimmy Gannet!